DEEP TROUBLE

As he dove for the river bottom, desperately trying to get as much water between himself and all that showering sludge as possible, Longarm heard and felt ominous plunging splashes all around. He was far enough away, he hoped, to be out of range of really big chunks of flying steamboat. His blindly groping fingers dug into soft slimy mud. He tried to grip the bottom of the river to no avail. But he knew that even as he was running out of air, the current was sweeping him ever further. . . .

TABOR EVANS

LONGARM

AND THE
BOUNTY HUNTRESS

J

JOVE BOOKS, NEW YORK

LONGARM AND THE BOUNTY HUNTRESS

A Jove Book / published by arrangement with
the author

PRINTING HISTORY
Jove edition / April 1991

ISBN: 0-515-10547-3

Jove Books are published by The Berkley Publishing Group,
200 Madison Avenue, New York, New York 10016.
The name "JOVE" and the "J" logo
are trademarks belonging to Jove Publications, Inc.

PRINTED IN THE UNITED STATES OF AMERICA

10 9 8 7 6 5 4 3 2 1

LONGARM

AND THE
BOUNTY HUNTRESS

Chapter 1

The bank robbers who picked the middle of a Wednesday morning as the best time to hit the Mountain Savings and Loan near 17th and Blake were too slick by half for their own intended evil.

It was true as a rule of thumb that traffic at that time should be as thin as it ever got in downtown Denver during banking hours. It was just as true that not even Deputy U.S. Marshal Custis Long left for work quite that late in the morning, and that even if he *had* been en route to the federal building from his furnished digs on the unfashionable side of Cherry Creek, his customary course called for crossing the creek via the Larimer Street Bridge and pausing for breath and some coffee with apple pie and chili con carne at an all-night beanery a good two city blocks wide of the holdup in progress.

But on this particular Wednesday morn, still suffering the effects of a Tuesday night that had turned out mighty odd, Longarm was moving east along 17th from the Union Depot, cussing himself in advance for the cussing he knew he'd be in for at the office, when he noticed a young cowboy, or so it would seem, holding the reins of his own and four, count 'em, four other cow ponies, smack in front of the Mountain Savings and Loan.

It was a free country. Many another mid-morning strider, including at least one copper-badged roundsman from the Denver P.D., had passed by the innocent-looking rustic to consider, if they considered at all, how close Blake Street was to the Denver Stockyards. Longarm considered that too. It was the middle of June. But roundups were either in the spring or fall, and as he knew from his own misspent youth chasing cows for richer gents, nobody else in the cattle industry got paid any damned day but the last damned day of the month.

As he casually broke stride to get the recess of an empty shop with a For Rent sign in its dusty window to his back, with a filled-to-the-brim watering trough between him and whatever was up on the far side of the street, Longarm fished out a three-for-a-nickel cheroot and lit it, his natural hand movements disguising the way he cleared the tail of his tobacco-tweed frock coat from the grips of his .44-40, worn cross-draw on his left hip.

The young and innocent-looking cuss across the way didn't seem to notice him. Longarm figured that was fair. He was busting a gut trying not to look as if *he'd* noticed toad squat either. The odds were ten to one the kid was simply minding the stock for, say, a boss on honest banking business. But what the hell, there was always the outside chance, and even if he was playing the fool, Longarm knew his own boss, the firm but fair Marshal Billy Vail, would accept the word of a fellow peace officer about suspicious characters before he'd call him a liar.

So Longarm stood there, smoking, and wishing the riders that went with all those saddles would get on out there so he could be on his way before it got so late that nothing he might do or say figured to justify it. A stray whiff of morning breeze made Longarm's smoke taste just awful till he figured out what in thunder stunk like so. Larimer and most of the east-west numbered streets had gotten at least a nominal paving of hot-rolled tar since the original paving of creosote and coal oil had been worn through to virgin 'dobe and horseshit. The paving crew had made it further along Blake than he'd figured. He wished they were in sight so

2

he could have something more interesting to watch than one paint pony shitting in the company of four others and one suspicious character. The young-looking cuss was yawning now. Longarm resisted the impulse to do the same and muttered, "I'll bet you never wound up aboard a train with a fat lady instead of out to Arvada with a trimmer-figured orphan-asylum boss. I feared I was fixing to wind up in Boston with that Miss Hewitt when it was Miss Floyd I'd come calling on to begin with!"

A million years, or at least another couple of thoughtful drags on his cheroot, passed by and Longarm was sorely tempted to chuck it. There seemed no way anything but a mighty long discussion about bank loans and such could be transpiring yonder. Bank robbers and even sensible gents with honest business were supposed to damnit get in and get out. Another gent was coming along the walk in a more sissy outfit now. The rougher-dressed kid holding the ponies paid him no particular mind as he strode past and turned into the open doorway of the bank. Longarm grimaced and muttered, "Well, I'd say that about tears it. Only what are we supposed to tell Billy when he asks, as he surely will, how come we wasted all this time on Lord knows what without following up on it?"

So that was how come Longarm was halfway across the street, facing the bank, as three wild-eyed desperados wearing identical travel dusters and packing sixguns came busing out the door all at once, whooping and shooting as they came, as if to rattle any copper-badge who might be in sight.

But Longarm wasn't easy to rattle when he figured that was what you might be out to do. He whipped out his own .44-40 to fire first at the one holding the getaway ponies. So there went the getaway, the paint and a roan loping east towards the civic center whilst the other three tore west as sudden.

That left three of the gang still upright as well as outraged at the thought of all the walking the tall dark figure in front of them seemed out to put them through. But Longarm had expected their likely next moves well before any of them

3

had come unstuck enough to make any. So he sent one staggering back inside with a round just over the heart, folded another like a jackknife just above the one he'd dropped on the walk, and got off a parting shot that inspired a kicked-dog yip from the one whipping around the brick corner, sort of blurred by all the gunsmoke.

Since a suspicious character afoot in downtown Denver with a bullet in his ass made for chores the Denver P.D. could just as well handle, Longarm ran on, flattened out against the bricks just to one side of the gaping door, and reloaded as he called out, "You all inside the bank: The situation out here is under control and I'm the law, federal. So what's going on in there?"

A frightened feminine voice called back, "They just held us up, ah, Sheriff. You say you lawmen caught them all, though?"

Longarm was too slick to discuss numbers as he replied. He could count too. He said, "That's about the size of it. Why don't you come out and tell us all about it, ma'am?"

There was a pregnant pause. Then she answered, weakly, "I can't. I'm, ah, wounded. We're *all* wounded in here. They were waiting for Mister Neary to arrive so he could open the safe-deposit vault and then they, ah, made sure none of us could go for help."

Longarm said, "That sounds reasonable, until you add up the number of gunshots within a quarter mile of here this morning. Since I see we got a standoff here, it might save time if the one last outlaw spoke for his own fool self. What do you figure on getting outta scaring all those banking folk like this, boy—an extra year at hard if I know Judge Dickerson worth spit?"

A more masculine but no less worried voice called back, "I don't want to talk to any judge. For there ain't no deal any judge can ever offer an old boy with my record, if you take my meaning."

"Who might you be and who did you kill?" asked Longarm.

His unseen hostage-taker replied with a somewhat braver sneer, "That's for me to know and you to find out. Suffice it

4

to say, they can only hang you once and they has to catch you first. So here be my terms. I want me a buckboard out front. Then I want everyone to back off so's me, my hostages, and enough of this swell money they just handed over can light out unmolesticated."

Before Longarm could reply Sergeant Nolan of the Denver force came around the corner, whistled at the bodies on the walk, and declared, "I might have known it was you, Longarm. I have a couple of me own covering the back. What have we got left inside?"

Longarm replied in a loud but conversational tone, "One, if I can count saddlehorns. He's holding hostages. I sent one of his pals reeling off down Blake with a bullet where it feels really embarrassing. Did he get through you and your'n?"

Nolan moved closer, drawing his own .45, as he growled, "Surely you jest. Paddy Coyne was the roundsman who came running this way when he heard the gunplay. The fool tried to pull free when Coyne collared him. Never do that to a Connemara man when he's holding a billy in his great hand. The outlaw lad may live, in the end, but he won't be awake in the near future. What might the one left be after asking to let his captives go?"

Longarm told Nolan about the buckboard and added, "I don't think he means to let anyone go. Not until he's long gone himself, at any rate, and you know as well as I that we can't go along with that notion!"

"I swear I mean to kill 'em and toss 'em out to you, one by one!" the outlaw inside called out.

Another feminine voice whimpered, "Oh, do as he asks, good sirs! He'll surely kill us all if you don't do just as he demands!"

Nolan shot Longarm a questioning glance. The taller federal lawman grimaced and said, "Yep, he's got at least *two* females to bargain with. Both of 'em young and scared shitless, if I'm any judge of the species."

Nolan swore under his breath and said, "I don't like this either way. But what if we was to go along with him just enough to get him and them darling gorls out in the open? Sure and it's early in the day. Where could he get with his

5

cash and captives that we couldn't be after following by broad day and all?"

Longarm shook his head and growled, "Better the devil we know than the devil we don't. Would you really want to peg a shot at a wagon load of hostages bouncing lickety-split through either the town or fairly heavily settled country betwixt here and the Front Range?"

Nolan sighed and said, "I would not. But what if he makes good on his threat and shoots even one of them in there and all?"

Longarm shrugged. "That'll make it on *his* head, not yours or mine. Give in an inch to an outlaw's terms and whatever happens after that is your fault as well as his, see?"

Nolan apparently did. Then they were joined by a precinct captain and, worse yet, Reporter Crawford of the *Denver Post*.

Neither newcomer was dumb enough to expose himself to fire from the gaping doorway, of course. As they flattened out by Longarm and the burly Sergeant Nolan, the man inside fired a shot, hopefully just for attention, and yelled, "I meant what I said about pitching 'em out to you one at a time, grievous injured if not entirely dead, hear?"

"We're studying on your kind offer," Longarm called back, soothingly. One of the captive girls still bawled like someone was branding her on both tits while Longarm and Nolan filled the newcomers in on the standoff.

The precinct captain said, "Getting him and those captives out in the open ought to at least let us see what we're doing, right?"

Longarm shook his head and said, "Wrong, Captain. Seeing what you're doing don't count for shit when you got no control over what might happen next. So far, what we got us here is pure standoff. Let him outta that box, gun in hand with Lord only knows what twisted plans, and folks who ain't even in on this so far could wind up dead!"

The unseen outlaw called out, "I'm tired of talking. I'm going to start counting. When I get done counting I reckon I'll start with this bitty blond gal. She ain't as pretty as the

6

dark-headed one and I'm tired of listening to her weeping and wailing, hear?"

The police officer yelled, "Hold your fire! You say you want a buckboard? A dray won't do?"

"Shit, I'll take an ice cart, long as it's got room in it for all of us and, oh, yeah, I'd rather have a mule team out front than one horse of any color!" The outlaw chortled.

Longarm stared soberly at the uniformed appeaser and softly growled, "That was really bright of you. Now that you've given that son of a bitch an inch I got me another mile to take in. Men hardly ever give up unless they figure they got no choice. You just offered him a choice. Don't do that no more. I mean it."

The precinct captain blinked in surprise and blustered, "The hell you say! I'll have you know I'm the ranking peace officer here, Long!"

Longarm favored him with a cold gray look and told him, flatly, "Don't fuck with me. You can only eat the apple a bite at a time, and the only asshole I got time for right now is the one inside."

Before the outraged local lawman could reply Longarm turned back to the doorway and called, "You're not getting nothing from this child but your life, guaranteed, if you'd like to toss out your gun and follow with some sky in your dainty hands, pilgrim."

"You're full of it, and I'm counting with my gun aimed right at this ugly blonde!" the unseen other snarled.

The unseen gal, ugly or not, wailed, "He's going to kill me, like he says, and I don't want to die, good sirs!"

Longarm didn't assure her the cuss was likely bluffing. As a lawman of some experience, he knew how many folk had been shot daring another damned fool to shoot. So he tried, instead, "If he harms one hair on your pretty little head, he knows he'll pay for it with considerable discomfort of his own. That's guaranteed too. Are you listening to me in there, pilgrim?"

The bank robber sounded almost as scared as the girl he was tormenting as he called back, "I hear you. Now tell me

7

what a man wanted for murder already has to lose, Lawman!"

Longarm chuckled and replied, "You may be hearing, but you don't seem to be listening. I said I'd feel honorbound to take you in alive and well, provided you left them innocent banking folk in the same condition. It ain't for me to say what might or might not happen at your trial. Even if you don't get off, they'll still let you live Lord only knows how long, and then even if they hang you, they'll do do so considerate as they know how."

The bank robber snarled, or whimpered, it was tough to tell. "You don't paint a very cheersome picture, Lawman."

To which Longarm answered in a grimmer tone, "Try this one then. Try dying sooner, closer, with let's say one round in your bladder and both kneecaps shot off. You know as well as we do that once you gun the first hostage, there's just no way we can get out of coming in there to break up such a party, don't you?"

The literally desperate desperado tried, "I swear I'll nail the first one through yonder door."

Longarm chuckled fondly and replied, "That ought to put the rest of us you *don't* wing in a right friendly mood. It was back East, near a place called Shiloh, I first saw a man take a round in the bladder. In the end a kindly sergeant took pity on the poor screaming cuss and shot him in the head for us. Lord knows how long he'd have gone on carrying on like that, left to his own devices and considerable discomfort. You see, old son, your kidneys keep on making all this acid even with the bladder to store it busted open just above your, ah, never mind with ladies present."

There was a scream of pure terror, hopefully from one of the female captives in there. Then the trapped outlaw said, "What if I make you boys kill me flat out? I always said a blaze of glory had to have hanging beat all hollow."

Longarm replied in a thoughtful tone, "You might manage to get killed right out, assuming you took me and my, ah, guarantee with you. Did I mention the effects of a .44–40 on the human kneecap or even an elbow joint just now? You've doubtless bumped your funny bone often enough

8

to picture a bullet hitting that same nerve. The one in your knee runs deeper as well as way bigger but the effect is much the same, in spades."

The gunslick inside didn't answer. A fresh face above the familiar blue uniform of the Denver P.D. came around the corner to tell Nolan his pard in the alley out back wanted to know how long they'd be stuck there, damnit. Nolan had just told the roundsman to get his ass back to where it had been posted when an Army Schofield .45 clattered on the sandstone just outside the bank entrance.

Longarm called, "So far so good. Let's see the rest of you!" And then a tall drink of water with scared rabbit eyes came out into the morning light, hands high and wearing a duster too short and a Texas hat too big for him. The precinct captain snapped, "I arrest you in the name of the law and the city of Denver!" and moved in to collar the cuss as Longarm shouted, "No! It ain't him!" too late to do a thing for the poor cuss in the ill-fitting duster and high-button shoes as three rapid-fire rounds of .45–28 Short slammed into his back and pitched him headfirst into the thundergasted police captain!

As they both went down in a bewildered tangle Longarm was already whipping around the jamb of the wide doorway in a dry-mouthed crouch. As he crabbed sideways to make his outline less inviting against the gloom away from the doorway, he noticed he was still alive but having a hell of a time noticing anything else in the tricky light and haze of gunsmoke. He shouted, "Everybody on my side hit the floor, *poco tiempo*!" as he moved in past the one he'd dropped before just inside the entrance. Then a blinding pillar of fire, or sunlight coming through a partways open doorway somewhere in the back of the bank, encouraged him to peg a shot that way for luck and follow after it at a long-legged lope. As he passed a gal peeking out from under a desk at him she sobbed, "He's out in the alley now! Did he kill Mister Hart?"

Longarm didn't have time to answer or decide whether she'd been the pretty one or the ugly one. He hit the back door running and burst out into the sun-drenched alleyway just in time to peg yet another round at a figure running out the far end in high-heeled boots and ragged-ass jeans. A copper-badge, sprawled closer but still breathing, yelled, "He got me, the son of a bitch! Don't let him get away!"

So Longarm kept running, even faster than the tricky bank robber could with at least two rounds in him and all that fresh-poured Trinidad tar gumming up his fancy border boots now.

For the desperado had run smack into that paving job on Blake Street, scaring the liver and lights out of the work crew who'd never been told the job might entail spreading and rolling tar under fire.

That was doubtless why they'd all lit out in every direction, leaving Blake Street from curb to curb to the fleeing outlaw and the lawman chasing him.

Unable to run or, hell, walk fast enough to matter with his boot heels stuck in sticky tar, the leg-shot outlaw hunkered down in the center of the street to draw a two-handed bead on Longarm, who just as naturally dropped to one knee behind a couple of hopefully filled ash cans to return the favor. But then he had an even neater notion.

The paving crew had run off. The big steamroller they'd used to flatten that Trinidad tar with had been abandoned with more haste than concern for public safety. So it was still rolling, slow but sure, and Longarm held his fire as he saw that, sure enough, the large mass of hot steam-powered mental was aimed just right.

The outlaw became aware of the awful fate creeping in on him from behind in time to almost spoil the fun. Letting out a frightened honk, he put another round into the ash can in front of Longarm as he tried to spring back up, found out how tough that could be with a bullet in one thigh, and made an awesome amount of noise as the big steamroller slowly spread him flat as a pancake over a considerable area of Blake Street.

Longarm caught up with the steamroller at a walk, reloading his sidearm as he did so, and climbed up to disengage the forward gear and shut the steam throttle just as Nolan and Reporter Crawford came around the corner to join him. The newspaper man called out, "The captain wasn't hurt bad and that banker might make it. What about the smart-ass who shoved a hostage out in his own place and . . . Jesus H. Christ! What's that spread so wide and flat back yonder, Longarm?"

As Sergeant Nolan figured out what that mess had to be, and made the sign of the cross, Longarm shrugged and said, "They're going to have to lay at least another inch of tar atop him if they mean to pave this fool street permanent. One of your own is down in the alley behind the bank, Nolan. We'd best see what can be done for him. Ain't a thing anyone can do for *this* flat-faced son of a bitch!"

As Longarm and Nolan headed back into the alley, Crawford fell in on the far side, chortling. "I can see the headline they'll want to run above my byline, you interesting cuss. Longarm Paves Blake Street with Bandit! How does that sound to you?"

"Awful," Longarm replied, adding in a soberly sincere way, "I'd be obliged if you was to play my part in this morning's affair sort of modest, Crawford. By rights us federal deputies ain't supposed to horn into such purely local matters, see?"

Crawford frowned and said, "Not really. Wasn't it you, just now, telling a local precinct captain off when he tried to tell you he was in command here?"

Longarm nodded but explained, "I had to. He was going about it all wrong. That still don't change the simple fact that he was right about the Denver P.D. having the juris-diction."

Crawford whistled softly and said, "I can see why you want us to hide your light under the bushel basket! The powers that be in this town could get sore as hell if they were to think you and Marshal Vail were out to steal their glory!"

To which Longarm could only reply, "I just said that."

Chapter 2

The mining camp of Cherry Creek had gotten too fancy for casual gunplay since they'd changed its name to Denver and commenced to pave half its streets with Trinidad tar. So between one infernal form to fill out and another, the day was more than half-shot by the time Longarm finally made it to work that morning, at around three in the afternoon.

Young Henry, the tough enough but prissy-looking kid who played the typewriter out front, told Longarm their boss, Marshal William Vail of the Denver District Court, was out of the office on serious chores of his own. Then Henry spoiled it all by adding, "He said to make sure you were here when he got back," before Longarm could go look for Vail in vain at this late hour.

As Longarm eased down aboard the chesterfield sofa provided for the general public, Henry asked if he'd seen the afternoon editions of the *Rocky Mountain News* and *Denver Post*. Longarm sighed and reached for a smoke as he replied, "I have, and I was cross as hell with my pals on the *Post* till I noticed how comically the *News* covered events of this morning."

Henry nodded soberly and observed, "Betwixt Mark Twain and Bret Harte, nobody reports the news these days without a pinch of barnyard humor. To read this afternoon's *News*, a body would think we had Black Jack Slade smoking up the Overland Trail this morning, and how come you were down around Seventeenth and Blake at that hour, in case the boss yells at me about that again."

Longarm didn't like to lie any more than he liked to kiss and tell. So he took his time lighting his cheroot, and made certain he'd shaken the match all the way out before he softly said, "I was on my way to work, of course."

To which Henry shot back, with a knowing look, "You sure went out of your usual ways then, considering you'd have already been late reporting in if you'd been leaving your furnished digs across the creek or a certain widow woman's back gate up to Capitol Hill that long after sunrise, right?"

Longarm smiled sheepishly and confided, "I was a mite surprised to find myself aboard a milk train at sunrise, if the truth be known, Henry."

"You went *train riding* last night?" asked the clerk with a frown.

Longarm nodded and said, "Ask me no names and I'll tell you no fibs. I reckon it's safe to say I'd planned meat balls at Romano's and *The Fair Maid Of Croissy* at the Apollo Playhouse with another gal entirely."

"That rich young widow, the matron at the orphan asylum, or that new barmaid at the Parthenon?" asked Henry, who'd obviously been down the hall jawing with the female typewriter players of late.

Longarm blew smoke out both nostrils and growled, "I told you to ask me no names, you biddy hen in britches. Suffice it to say the one I'd made the date with was stuck with an extra night shift neither of us had been warned about. I'd gone and hired us a surrey in the meantime and, seeing as she had this friend as needed a lift to Union Depot, it seemed only Christian to haul her ass and baggage along."

Henry laughed and said, "I know how the rest of it goes. Had she been any prettier or, come to study on it, uglier, those outlaws might have gotten away with robbing that bank this morning."

13

It would have been rude to say crude things about the enthusiastic bumps and grinds of a fat girl who'd tried to make up for her obvious shortcomings with some long comings indeed. So Longarm just nodded agreeably and blew smoke rings till their boss stomped in, red faced and puffing disagreeably.

Marshal Vail was way older, shorter, and dumpier than either his clerk typist or senior deputy. A shrewd enough lawman both in his earlier days in the field and even now pushing papers, Billy Vail was one of those men who look more and more like bald babies as they get older. In this case, he was one that always seemed about to throw a screaming fit if he didn't get his way, damned sudden. So when Vail snapped at Longarm to tag along, the tall deputy simply rose to his considerable height to follow as Henry shot him a look midway between sympathy and "Now you're gonna get it!"

But once they were back in his darker oak-paneled inner sanctum, Vail simply waved Longarm to a seat across the cluttered desk from his own swivel chair, plopped his own ample rump down in his chair, and growled, "I just had a mighty long late lunch with the Denver D.A. I told him you'd done right, no matter what the Denver P.D. may have to say. Don't let that go to your one brain cell, though. Right is right, wrong is wrong, and you'd have been here where you belonged if only you'd pay attention to half the factory whistles going off in this town every morning. How in thunder do you manage to sleep through all the early morning din, as close to the railroad yards as you bunk, Longarm?"

Longarm said it wasn't easy as he absently glanced at the banjo clock on one wall. As if he'd read the younger lawman's mind old Vail said, "I'm sending you out in the field on an undercover chore. First things coming first, we've just about time to get you outta that baggy tweed outfit and gussied up proper for polite society afore the men's shop up on Tremont closes."

Longarm whistled softly and said, "You must want me gussied indeed if we're talking about such sissy shopping,

Billy. I doubt you could buy a shirt in such surroundings for less'n five dollars! But what's wrong with the outfit I got on? It's good enough to escort prisoners in and outta court down the hall, ain't it?"

Vail found the sheaf of papers he'd been rummaging for and rose again, saying, "Come on. I'll fill you in on the fly. All you have to know right now is that you'll never nail Lucky Lovelace looking half as much like a working stiff as you usually do."

Longarm got back up too, bouncing the name around in his skull a few times before he followed Vail back out, muttering, "I'd never lose track of a handle like Lucky Lovelace if it was attached to anything important. You say you want me to sneak up on this want in a five-dollar shirt?"

Vail told Henry to wait for him as he swept through the reception room with Longarm in tow. Out in the marble halls of the federal building Vail explained, "It ain't a matter of you sneaking in to get the drop on the cuss, murderous as some say he can be. You or any other peace officer worth his salt should be able to take the cowardly cuss. He's never yet won a face-to-face fight, or even *had* one, as far as we know."

They got to the stairwell. Billy Vail took his time moving down it as he continued. "The problem you or any other peace officer faces in regard to Lucky Lovelace is that nobody knows his face. Lord only knows the name he'll be traveling under, now that he's wanted, federal, as Ethelred a.k.a. Lucky Lovelace."

Longarm dropped his smoked-down cheroot in a handy fire bucket as they passed it, asking what else they had to single this lucky rascal out in a crowd.

Vail grimaced and said, "Damn near nothing. He describes as clean-cut and tastefully attired, of average height, weight, and build. Some witnesses recall his eyes as gray, like your'n, whilst others feel sure they're hazel. His hair's either dark brown or black, whether he dyes it or not. He speaks with an educated Midwestern accent. How do you like it so far?"

Longarm swore softly and replied, "Get to the part about my having to trail him dressed like a pimp, Billy."

Vail chuckled at the picture but explained. "Prosperous stockman with sporting instincts was more what I had in mind. Lovelace is said to shun the company of riverboat tinhorns as well as strangers who might be wearing a badge under a cheaper cut of cloth than you usually meet riding first class up or down the Big Muddy."

As they crossed the street and swung toward Tremont, Longarm frowned thoughtfully. "You want me *that* far out in the field, for Pete's sake?"

Vail nodded. "Somewhere betwixt Great Falls and Saint Lou, as far as anyone can figure. When he ain't killing federal employees, Lucky Lovelace is slicker than your average riverboat gambler. They come close to nailing him in Cairo a few days ago. So right now he could be on the Mississippi, Missouri, Ohio, or, hell, Tennessee. But you and me are betting on the Missouri. Tell me why, if you're so smart."

Longarm grabbed his shorter boss by one arm to keep him from having his fly unbuttoned by the wheel-hub of a passing dray. Only then did he feel up to replying. "That's easy. I noticed the time you sent me to find out who'd been dumping all that U.S. mail in the Big Muddy. The railroads have dulled the shine of the steamboat's shining times. I doubt they'll ever move heavy freight cheaper by way of land than water, but when it comes to fast passenger service, the railroads have steam-boating beat all hollow."

Then he added, "Save for where their ain't no rails laid yet, along the upper reaches of the Big Muddy. That's how come the crooks messing up the mail service up near Great Falls had us all so worried a spell back, remember?"

Vail said, "I'm glad *you* do. Important gents with time on their hands and money to bet in a friendly little game can still be found, traveling first class, on the shallow-draft sternwheelers up above Saint Lou, or leastways Omaha. Where's that infernal haberdash shop? Oh, yonder's the sign, bitty and modest like they have over the water in London Town."

Longarm strode beside his somewhat breathless boss, saying soothingly, "Don't get your bowels in an uproar, Billy. They ain't about to close this early, and even if they was, you haven't explained exactly why we're so hell-bent on making me look even more like a sissy than I already have to since President Hayes and Lemonade Lucy took over in Washington."

Vail called him a blamed fool.

As they forged on toward the high-toned haberdashery Longarm insisted, "You just said this Lovelace cuss ain't much of a fighter, and once I'm on the same sternwheeler with him, where's he supposed to run to that I can't follow, dressed comfortable or not?"

Vail said, "I was coming to that. You have to spot Lovelace before you can arrest him. That ain't easy when a man looks much the same as anyone else. I told you he'll be traveling first class in the company of gents too important for you or even me to just search for identification, and in any case, Lovelace may have plenty of identification whilst some rich dude such as Bet A Million Grits—"

"That's Gates. Bet A Million Gates," Longarm said, interrupting. "He peddles bobwire, a heap of bobwire, when he ain't offering to bet a million on most any sporting event you can think of."

Vail sniffed and said, "Yeah, him too. My point is that Lovelace keeps company with beef barons, industrial giants, and such that you can't just throw down on by mistake if you value your job, or mine. You got to ease in Apache-style and make sure you got the right man before you flash your badge and cuff him secure. The U.S. deputy he killed in Cairo didn't. Lucky had a whore pistol in one boot."

They were almost to the entrance of the haberdashery now. Knowing how awkward it might be to converse about such matters in front of a snooty cuss with tape and tailor's chalk, Longarm stopped Vail on the walk out front to demand, "How *am* I supposed to separate this wanted goat from all them delicate-natured sheep, even wearing sheep's clothing, Billy?"

Vail said, "You'll have time to study all we know about Lovelace on the way, once we get you looking less cow. Like I said, he can pass for a gent of quality with otherwise-average dimensions. After that, he does have some unusual personal habits you'll find in the folder of carbon papers Henry will have ready with your travel vouchers. Meanwhile we got to get you close enough to him and his fancy friends to observe 'em unobserved. If Lovelace suspects for a second that he might not be surrounded by his favored prey, he only has to pull in his horns and sit in the corner like Little Jack Horner. You have to catch him in the act of ordering food and drink or dealing cards. They say he's partial to tea with lemon, no cream or sugar, and likes 'em to cut the crusts off his white bread sandwiches, the priss."

Longarm grimaced. "Lot's of rich gents put on fancy table manners, whether they started out with them or not. You say we got something on his double-dealing?"

Vail pursed his lips and replied, "He's never been caught in the act of cheating. That don't mean a man who wins so consistent wins by luck alone, despite his nickname. He signs and shoots right-handed, like most of us. He deals left-handed. It's the only left-handed thing he's ever been known to do. I figure he started out a southpaw who was forced to do right and then—"

"It works another way," Longarm said, interrupting. "Tossing cards good enough with your left hand might help a dealer reading invisible markings on the backs of those cards with his right thumb."

Vail sighed. "Might have known you'd know how to cheat at cards too. If you're right, it's even worse. I don't see how you'd ever get a naturally right-handed man to give away left-handed leanings he just don't have! Your only hope will be to gain his confidence and get him to let his guard down. Let's get you spruced up to look less like Longarm and more like Bet A Million Long, the Cattle King of Colorado."

Longarm followed Vail inside, muttering, "I'd rather play Buffalo Bill in snow-white buckskins and a big sombrero. But there's one thing I don't follow about all this flimflammery, Billy. What in thunder has this Lucky Lovelace done to justify all the expenses of this here extensive manhunt?"

Vail looked uncomfortable and said, "I told you. He's a riverboat man who shot an arresting officer, federal, in Cairo. Afore that, he back-shot an Indian agent on the Memphis levee after a discussion of the game they'd just enjoyed coming down the river. There ain't nothing all that complicated about the case, save for what the wanted man looks like."

Longarm scowled and, ignoring the sure-enough prissy clerk mincing their way, demanded, "What's the weanie, Billy? Since when has the Denver District sent a deputy with my seniority that far out, undercover, just to collar a back-shooting tinhorn? What else has Lovelace done as makes his capture so important to this here department?"

The clerk had stopped a few feet away, bewildered by the heat of their exchange. Vail waved him on in, saying, "Mister Featherstone, I want you to dress this cowboy as close as you can to a Harvard grad with a gold mine. Just make sure you do it sudden. For we want him out of town before a certain son of a bitch on the Denver P.D. makes up his mind whether to press charges or die from a flesh wound."

Then, nodding at the thundergasted Longarm, Vail added, "That's right. I *don't* care if you catch Lovelace or not. But you may as well be doing *something* useful whilst we have you well away from the office for as long as it takes me to calm things down at City Hall."

Chapter 3

Longarm had reasoned, and Vail had agreed, that anyone departing Cairo by steamboat after gunning another lawman would have made it at least as far upstream as Omaha by this time, assuming he'd hopped a vessel headed up that particular river. All bets were off if the murderous mystery man had lit out up the Ohio or down the Mississippi. No passenger packets were even trying on the Tennessee this late in the slack water of high summer, and while there was still some high-toned steamboat traffic on the other rivers mentioned, the best bet was still the upper Missouri. For the northern High Plains were still shy of rail or, hell, dirt roads. But all that open range was where the next big boom figured to transpire, now that so many buffalo and horse Indians were down and the price of beef was up.

Meanwhile, rail transportation still had steamboating beat by miles where there were any rails at all. So along about sundown Longarm left Denver aboard the Omaha-bound Night Flier, realizing he'd been sitting at this very table in this very club car exactly twenty-four hours before, playing tickle-toes with a plump but pretty little thing in that very chair which now stood, damnit, empty.

At least he got to nurse a schooner of Anchor beer this evening, since he wasn't called upon to order anything more suited to sipping in female company. The fancy new duds Billy Vail had charged to the taxpayers in the cause of justice were still wrapped in fancy tissue paper and packed away for safekeeping as he let more railroad soot and tobacco ash mothproof his ready-made brown tweeds and good-enough Stetson, cleaned and blocked since the last time anyone had shot it off his fool head. Billy Vail had insisted on a porkpie hat of pearl gray felt with an English label and for-gawd's-sake piping around the wide but coyly curled brim. Longarm hated that hat, even though he'd only tried it on once in front of that pier glass.

His boss had insisted, and Longarm had been forced to agree, nobody would ever take a man in such an asshole hat for a country boy who'd resided in the West more than, say, six weeks. He'd promised Vail he'd get a haircut and have them splash some stink-pretty on him before he changed into the new sissy shirt and three-piece suit of robin's-egg-blue broadcloth. Had it been up to old Billy alone, Longarm would have wound up dressed even flashier. It had been a bitch convincing the older lawman that a man who dressed a mite sedately as well as prosperously would be in better shape if night fighting or tailing became involved.

As darkness fell and the already tedious prairie scenery out yonder got even less interesting to gaze at, Longarm broke out the manila dossier Henry had prepared for him on Ethelred a.k.a Lucky Lovelace, if that was the rascal's name.

Longarm doubted that as soon as he read where a man calling himself Lovelace had stiffed the purser of the *Robert E. Lee* for passage up to Memphis, lo, these several years back. Convincing one Southern gentleman you were another Southern gentleman, and then breaking your word when it came time to make good on that money order waiting on you in Memphis, was a swell way to make sure you were remembered on or about the *Robert E. Lee*. You wouldn't want to sign the passenger list of the *Natchez* with the handle of anyone who'd broken his word to a purser either, come to study on it.

"He can talk like a graduate of V.M.I. as well as like a

21

well-spoken Midwesterner," Longarm decided, half aloud.

To which a dulcet female voice replied, almost as softly, "Were you by any chance addressing me, good sir?"

Longarm glanced up from the dossier to find himself locking eyes with a gal sitting under a big picture hat at the next bitty table. He started to inform her with a sheepish smile that he was only a mite senile, now that he'd never see thirty again. Then he wondered why he'd want to say anything dumb as that. For she was somewhere in *her* middle thirties, give or take a few adventures, and after that it kept getting better. She was a vision of mature and worldly beauty with her inky black hair worn in a widow's peak above intelligent brows and wide-set eyes of cornflower blue. He had no complaints about the rest of her either. Her black silk bodice was tasteful but just a tad too tight for the figure it was no doubt meant to reveal. Better yet, he felt sure he'd seen her somewhere before. Recently. Knowing how dumb it would sound to ask, "Haven't I seen you somewhere before?" he settled for, "I was thinking out loud about someone else I'm supposed to catch up with. I didn't see you sit down beside me just now, which only goes to show how engrossed I was with somebody way less enchanting to look at, ma'am."

She nodded soberly and said, "I couldn't help wondering what you saw in that other young lady last night. But I must say the two of you put on a good act. I'd have never spotted you for what you have to be if you hadn't boarded the same train two nights in a row. Where's your fat sidekick, up forward, covering approaches to the mail car?"

Longarm closed the manila folder with a thin smile and went along with whatever game they were playing, for now. He said, "Matter of fact, we parted friendly this side of Grand Island, when the train paused to jerk boiler water at Kearney and . . . Just what are you accusing me of, ma'am, if it ain't molesting fat ladies?"

She dimpled demurely and confided, "I just said the two of you put on a good act. You had the Pullman porter convinced you were, ah, you know, up in that forward compartment. Who are you working for, Pinkerton or the U.P. line itself?"

He stared all about as if seeking some damned service as he told her, "I generally know who I'm jawing with before I tell 'em all that much about my own bad habits, ma'am. But for openers, I'd answer to Custis Long from West-By-God Virginia, and I'll be proud to buy you a drink of your choice, whether you'd like me to know more about you or not."

One of the colored kids helping the barkeep was on his way over now, as the brunette in the big black hat confided, "I think I'd like to be called Aura Lee for now, if it's all the same with you."

He nodded soberly and said, "I admire your taste in music. Both sides sang about you during the war. Last I heard the West Point cadets have changed the name of your song to 'Army Blue' so's they can sing it at graduation parties. What's your pleasure when it comes to liquid refreshment, Miss Aura Lee?"

She smiled and allowed a teeny-weeny julep, easy on the ice and forget the mint, might help settle her tummy after the dreadful supper they'd served up forward earlier.

He told the club car attendant to bring him more needled beer as well, and repressed the temptation to ask why in thunder she'd ordered supper aboard a train while it was still standing in the Denver yards. But even as the question was forming in his head, Longarm recalled this particular night train started down El Paso way, with Denver only one of its main stops. So naturally, a gal sort of living aboard the fool train as it plied its way back and forth between Omaha and El Paso . . . Raised some mighty interesting questions indeed.

She wasn't a railroad dick (dickess?). Neither she nor the Pullman porter she'd checked with would have been fooled about him unless, bless his hide, the porter had known who he really was and held out on an inquisitive female passenger in no way connected with the railroad.

He'd found out as much as he had by playing his own cards close to his vest and letting her show off how slick she was. So he busied his mouth with the beer he already had as they waited for their order.

The train rumbled on through the night a spell. He was able to ride silent longer than your average female, and she'd started out more proddy. So he wasn't too surprised when she suddenly blurted out, "I'd be willing to cut you in if you'd be willing to help me *get* the slippery cad!"

Longarm smiled thinly and replied, "Might have known you was a bounty huntress, Miss Aura Lee. No offense, but you're dressed too refined for a Pullman plaything, and who'd play cards on a train with a stranger female of any appearance? Which state or territory issued your private detective license and who are we after, for doing what?"

She didn't answer right off. The attendant had returned to Longarm's table with the two drinks. Aura Lee slid her trim rump gracefully from the chair she'd been in to another directly facing Longarm's. As the club car crewman turned away she reached for her julep, saying, "My hunting license was issued by El Paso County, Texas, and as far as I know it's recognized most anywhere I'd want to hunt. I've been riding this same train back and forth for nigh a week, in hopes of nailing a confidence man who works this line, preying on unescorted but prosperous-looking passengers of the distaff persuasion."

Longarm clinked glasses with her and observed, "You're a tad too good-looking to attract such gents, no offense. Even if you weren't, I don't see how he'd ever move in on you now, seeing you wouldn't look all that unescorted to any Casanova casing the cars for his usual prey."

She took a small sip from her glass before she demurely replied, "I know what he looks like. The lady he wronged would as soon have him dead as alive, and you'll never guess where I'm carrying a dear little .32 nine-shooter."

Longarm whistled softly. "Where you're packing a lethal weapon ain't half as important as the cuss you mean to use it on, ma'am. I'd be the first to agree a confidence man who preys on women deserves to die. But I fear the laws against such behavior fail to include capital punishment. Could I see the warrant you're packing on the rascal, before you go puncturing anyone with .32 slugs?"

She looked a mite flustered and confessed, "I don't have any writ issued by any court, yet. I'm operating on the, ah, formal complaint of a private citizen."

He shook his head. "You're skating on ice so thin you could pass for Jesus crossing the Jordan. You'd best tell me the whole tale, and then I'll tell you if you can even slap faces this far from Texas."

She sighed. "Once upon a time there was a no-longer-young but still warm-natured woman, the widow of a wealthy Texas *ranchero*, traveling aboard this very train on a business trip to Omaha."

He nodded. "I know they pack lots of beef in Omaha. I was there after other crooks a spell back. The one we're talking about picked up your client, the night ride being a lonesome one, and then what?"

Aura Lee wrinkled her pert nose and replied, "He took her for over a thousand dollars and, ah, other favors. I told you she was a warm-natured widow who seemed to be more respected in El Paso than any warm-natured woman really wants to be."

She took another sip and added, "After he'd had his wicked way with her, it seemed to the poor silly that they'd always known one another. He actually told her he loved her, their first night together, and she actually believed him. Have you ever heard a dumber tale of woe?"

Longarm nodded soberly and said, "Men in my line hear such sad stories all the time. In a world where nobody trusted anybody else, there'd be less need for our services."

He smiled wryly and felt obliged to continue. "On the other hand who'd want to live in such an unfriendly world? How did he get at her money after she'd let him get at *her*, knockout drops?"

Aura Lee shook her big hat and said, "She might not have been so cross with him, afterwards, if he'd simply ravaged and robbed her. No doubt the ravaging did her a world of good, and I just told you she was rich. The twelve hundred dollars he diddled her out of were not the inspiration for her anguish. What left her speechless with rage, once it sunk in, was that she'd *trusted* him. He'd given her some cock-and-bull story about not having enough on him to cinch a business deal when they got to Omaha and so—"

"You're right," Longarm said, cutting in. "She must have been lonely, and he must have been the bee's knees in a Pullman bunk."

Aura Lee fluttered her lashes and replied, "I believe they wound up in her private compartment. At any rate, they agreed to check discreetly into the same hotel, arriving by separate cabs. Needless to say, he never arrived at the hotel they'd agreed upon. It took her a while. She assumed at first he'd gone to that business meeting he'd mentioned. She had her own beef business to attend to. But by nightfall the penny dropped, and you know what they say about hell and a woman scorned."

Longarm nodded. "Remind me not to scorn any rich widows from El Paso. But I'm missing something here, Miss Aura Lee. If your client got diddled out of all that *dinero* days ago by a lying louse she met aboard this train, what are you doing aboard this train? At this late date, I mean. Surely you don't think he's expecting to meet her again, the same way?"

Aura Lee shook her head. "Riding back to Texas in a mood best described as ebony, she discovered more than one of the porters recalled her paramour as a frequent passenger. They recalled him fondly, as they would any other traveling man who tips well and makes few demands on the crew. He even uses the same name on his runs back and forth between Denver and Omaha. I thought that was dumber than it sounds until I pondered on his methods. This can't be the only railroad line he works, of course. But it would work best if the train crew knew him and addressed him as a familiar figure in front of a silly female he was out to impress, and how often would the same silly female be apt to board the same train?"

Longarm nodded. "Not often, unless she was a bounty huntress expecting the skunk to return to the scene of his stink. You was hoping he'd get on back there in Denver.

26

I'm sorry if I've disappointed you, Miss Aura Lee."

She had to raise her glass higher to get anything out of it now. As she lowered it back to the table she demurely replied, "It could have been worse. Nobody at all might have come aboard to keep me company and then where would I have been? If he's not waiting for this train in Omaha, I'll likely go mad with boredom by the time I get all the way back to El Paso, in vain, again!"

He chuckled. "I hope you won't take this wrong, ma'am. But you must be sort of new at bounty hunting. You just now said the rascal you're after rides regular betwixt Denver and Omaha. You could lay over in Denver and save yourself that useless five hundred miles to El Paso, both ways. Denver's cooler this time of the year, and with all due respect to El Paso, there's more for a lady with time on her hands to do in Denver, see?"

She shot him an arch look and replied, "I'm beginning to. What did you have in mind for me if I got off when this train gets back to your own home base?"

He smiled back. Then he sighed and said, "I won't be taking this train back to Denver for at least a few days, cuss my luck. I'm hunting someone a mite more serious, and if you haven't caught your con man by then you can assume he's on to you and riding another line. Meanwhile, going by what you've told me about the rascal, your best bet would be a citizen's arrest near either end so's you can hand him over to either the Omaha or Denver P.D. I can give you some names to avoid as well as those of copper-badges more likely to share our views on confidence men. Meanwhile, would you like me to order you some more shaved ice slightly tainted with bourbon?"

She laughed and said, "I've a better idea. I've a barely opened bottle of imported brandy in my compartment up forward, and there's enough ice in this silly glass to last me more drinks than a lady ought to sip in strange company."

He nodded soberly and signaled the attendant for their tab as he mused, half to himself, "It's a cool June night with ten or twelve hours of the same ahead of us. Do you reckon

27

we'll still feel like strangers by the time you've melted all that ice with hard liquor, Miss Aura Lee?"

She blushed becomingly, but didn't take her eyes from his as she softly replied, "I don't know. I can't wait to find out, can you?"

Chapter 4

In point of fact they were going at it hot and heavy long
before the ice in the glass she'd brought along had melted
away. Neither of them had been dumb enough to get really
drunk before getting down to more serious pleasures, and
since Longarm was almost as old and at least as experienced
as the mature woman of the world he'd picked up, or vice
versa, they undressed all the way, by tacit agreement, to
start out right after the first few ice-breaking moves on his
part, or vice versa.

As he mounted her atop the bedding of her firm bunk
against the Pullman windows, a rising prairie moon shed
just enough light in on their mingled bare flesh to per-
suade him she felt even better than she looked, and she
looked just swell spread-eagled under him like that with a
pillow under her shapely hips and her warm dark welcome
mat thrusting up to meet every stroke of his old organ-
grinder.

She must have liked what she could see, and feel, as well.
Locking her hands behind her head, she cranked her pretty
face up to stare down between their bare bellies, gasping,
"Ooh, I can spy it going in and out of me and it's so big,
Custis!"

He told her she had swell tits too. He wasn't just saying that to flatter her. He could tell that despite the way time's cruel shark had left its mark here and there on her pretty face, she'd managed to stay in almost tomboy shape, and there was a heap to be said for bedding a gal who sat a horse well, once she had her thighs gripping you in so friendly a way. She said she suspected *he* rode a lot too, once they'd come the first time, almost in unison, and she found he was still posting in her love saddle. She thought it was funny as hell when he said this was about the only time he preferred a trot to a less bouncy lope. He was glad she shared his easygoing attitude towards slap-and-tickle with a fellow traveler. He didn't say so, of course. That wasn't the way the game was played. Strangers on a train made neither crude remarks nor promises. That was likely what made for such pleasant memories of past romantic interludes with awfully nice folk whose exact names and other vital statistics eluded you as you thought back so fondly. Longarm had often thought, and proven it a few times by lingering a day too long, that many a whirling bitch, or son of a bitch, would always be remembered wistfully by some lucky stranger who'd never got to know them on the unfriendly side of the sheets.

He knew their train would roll into the Omaha yards at an ungodly hour unless they ran over at least a few cows or Indians, and that he'd sure look dumb creeping out of this lady's compartment as others getting off at Omaha were traipsing back and forth to the crapper. So he made up his mind not to fall asleep, and she found his notions of staying awake in bed with a beautiful woman delightful.

She said so, and came up with some interesting positions on her own. But when the train stopped for boiler water at Julesburg and she found herself taking it dog-style in front of a plate-glass window facing a well-lit loading platform, she dove flat as she could, begging him to pull down the shades for God's sake. So he did and, just as anxiously, lowered himself to park her firm bare cheeks and put it back where he, at least, thought it belonged.

She sobbed, "Don't you men ever think of anything else?"

30

To which he could only reply with a familiar pang, "Nope. We're all hairy beasts with dirty old dongs and a mad desire to prong school-girls, sheep, and such."

Then he swung his bare feet to the plush carpet, fumbled for his shirt on the carpet, and got out a smoke and some wax Mex matches as he assured her, "I'll be on my way as soon as we start up again. I'd leave sooner, but as you likely know from riding this line so often, the train crew's all over the place whilst they're jerking water and shoving stuff on and off."

She rolled over to prop herself up on one bare elbow, staring hurt and wide-eyed at him in the treacherous light, demanding, "That's it? Zim, zam, thank you, ma'am?"

He struck a light and soberly lit his smoke before he told her, "It was your notion to call it quits and send me back to my kennel. What were you expecting me to do, whimper for more now that you've had your own wicked way with an innocent boy like me?"

She laughed and said, "You fool. I found myself rutting like a barnyard beast on public display and . . . All right, it was dumb of me to blurt out that remark about men in general. Don't you ever say anything mean about women in general?"

He grinned sheepishly and said, "You're right. Men and women both deserve something better than they wind up in bed with. You want to share this smoke with me? I ain't got no hard feelings either way right now."

She said she'd be the judge of that, and made room for him to stretch out beside her, propped up for smoking, her brunette head nestled against his bare chest and one arm around her so he could fondle her too.

The train rolled on. By now he was feeling pleasantly sated, albeit not too sleepy yet, as he pondered the advantages and disadvantages of trying for a few winks in the time the night flier offered between there and Omaha. He'd just decided the forty winks and more would be worth the misery of such an early rising when he noticed she was either crying or bleeding all over his bare chest. He doubted she'd cut her throat or even bitten her tongue off. He knew that if he asked how come she was crying she'd tell him. So he didn't ask. He knew no man would ever grasp what got into women after a man had gotten into 'em if he lived to be a hundred. He was beginning to suspect that older gents like Billy Vail didn't slow down in their pursuit of the unfair sex because they couldn't get it up anymore. The older he got himself, the more he wondered why men bothered to get it up, considering how fleet the fucking and how protracted the fussing could get.

Naturally, since no woman believed any man born of mortal woman might not give a shit, Aura Lee sniffed and said, "I suppose you think I'm being a big silly. I mean, after all, I picked you up in the club car and it's not as if anyone made any promises, right?"

He took a drag on his cheroot, let it thoughtfully out, and said, "Once we get to Omaha I got to ask along the riverfront about any shallow-draft sternwheelers still taking first-class swells up the Big Muddy. Seeing you track down crooks abusing public transportation, might you know of any particularly fancy craft like so?"

She said she didn't know much about riverboats and then, as he'd hoped, she asked what they were talking about. So he told her about his federal badge and warrant for Lucky Lovelace. She seemed really interested until he got to the end. Then she sighed and said, "I'd be inclined to look for him amid as flush a crowd of prosperous sports as he could get in with. Wouldn't he sort of ask around on the landings, mayhap drawing some attention himself as he checks out passenger lists?"

He kissed the part of her hair and tweeked a nipple in a friendly way as he replied, "Bless you, child. That could be worth following up on. He lit out from Cairo in a hurry. Lord knows who or what might have been aboard the very next steamboat out. I'm hoping to beat him to Omaha. He may, like you say, take time to scout up better company, feeling safer that far upstream. If he's still running scared or, Lord help us, already further up the river . . . Well, we don't get 'em all."

She snuggled closer and said, "I wish you'd lay over in

32

Omaha with me at least a little while, Custis. Now that you've warned me I can't just gun Paul Henderson like the dirty dog he is, I confess I'm a bit edgy about having to take him to the Omaha law alive. What if he doesn't want to come? He's a big man, almost as big as you, but if you were with me when I caught up with him . . . "

Longarm ran the name Paul Henderson through his mental file as he snubbed out the spent cheroot. She'd said Henderson worked out of Denver. Longarm said, "He ain't wanted on anything federal. But once we get to Omaha I can put you in touch with some decent Omaha detectives I've worked with before, and if that don't work I'd best introduce you to the boss railroad dick of this line, Omaha being U.P. headquarters."

She kissed his wrist and placed his free hand where it could inspire them both, saying, "Goody. Might there be time for you to check into the Mayfair with me so's we can do it right at least once?"

He laughed and replied, "I got no complaints about the way you screw on a bunk bed, honey. But I got to set up headquarters somewhere in town till I get a line on Lovelace's present whereabouts, and by the way, the Mayflower's a mite better than the Mayfair if you're talking room service and lots of time in bed."

She said she surely was, and proved it by cocking one shapely thigh across him to spit herself sweetly on his freshly inspired erection. He laughed and said, "There I go acting like a dirty old man again!"

To which she could only reply, "You sure are, bless every horny inch of your depraved dong!"

Chapter 5

Aura Lee agreed the Mayflower offered more for the money than the Mayfair she usually checked into in Omaha, and wondered aloud why friends in Texas had given her such a steer. Longarm said it was as likely some Texican who'd enjoyed a stay at the Mayflower had mixed up the names. They sounded somewhat alike and both hotels were in about the same price range, albeit at opposite ends of Leavenworth Street.

They attracted little attention checking in by the dawn's early light with plenty of baggage. She still seemed to think it best if they booked adjoining rooms and register separately under the names their identification went with.

He didn't care. His office would pay hotel bills for him as long as he refrained from billing honeymoon suites, double occupancy, to the taxpayers. He didn't know how long he'd be in town in any case, and figured it best if his own baggage was where he could get at it day or night without disturbing a sleepyhead with an uncertain temper.

He needed a bath both before and after they tested the springs of her spiffy hotel bed. But he only changed his underwear, and put on the same old suit and a clean but careworn work shirt for his first scouting expedition. As he strode the sunny streets of Omaha, more than one cuss dressed even more cow cast a thoughtful glance at the way his coattails draped on his left side. But he had his badge and identification if any copper-badge got officious about the man-sized .44-40 he was wearing as sedately as possible.

He tried the boat landing at the foot of Douglas first. That was where one crossed to Council Bluffs on the far side of the river if the boat you were looking for didn't stop on the Omaha side. As early as it was, the day was shaping up warm and muggy. So a riverfront drinking establishment had set up some tin tables under an awning out front.

This early, the sun was still able to get at the green-painted tables and black-wire chairs. Longarm sat down on one such chair anyway, loosening his shoestring tie and removing his hat so he could fan his flushed face while observing the river and everything going on between him and it.

Nothing much was, at this hour. The Big Muddy flowed by the color and texture of chocolate milk. Out in midstream an uprooted cottonwood tree, a big one, bobbed along looking for trouble. He knew from some pleasant time in the company of an auburn-haired steamboat skipper who was, hopefully, married happily these days that such deadwood didn't cause much trouble unless or until a floating tree became a "snag" stuck on a shoal. Or worse yet, a "sawyer" or water-logged and grounded mass of timber that had one downstream end bobbing or "sawing" up and down in the current so that now a river pilot saw it and now he didn't. A sawyer coming up, as a flat-bottomed sternwheeler was passing over it, could do almost as much damage as a blown boiler. Nothing could do as *much* damage as a blown boiler. But an engineer with a lick of sense could keep a steamboat's boilers from blowing. Avoiding sawyers took more than skill. A good river pilot needed a sixth sense, and a little luck never hurt when the river was falling after a gully-washing rain that had torn at all the banks upstream.

An old cuss in a dirty shirt and spotless white apron came out with a push broom to catch Longarm sitting there. He said, "This ain't no public park, pilgrim. If you aim to set there, you're going to have to order something."

Longarm nodded soberly and replied, "I'd be proud to, if someone would only get his ass out here with a wine list or, failing that, a schooner of draft and what's the free lunch this morning?"

The old-timer snapped, "Too early for free lunch. A pint schooner will set you back a nickel out here under the luxurious new awning. We don't extend credit to strangers, if you take my meaning."

Longarm said he did, produced a whole quarter, and said he'd trust the old fart not to abscond with his change if someone around there could tell him a thing or two about the passenger service on the upper Missouri. The older man said he wasn't no damned ticket agent, and scooped up the quarter before Longarm could change his mind.

By the time he was back with the change and a pretty good pint of lager, Longarm was starting to regret his choice of vantage. Over on the far side a smudge of smoke was moving upstream against the bare cliffs that gave the town of Council Bluffs its name, Omaha being named for a fairly calm breed of Lakota, Nakota, or Dakota speakers, depending on how far west or east the infernal redskin was speaking.

By squinting hard against the morning glare Longarm could see that the towboat puffing all that smoke was pushing a couple of barges up the river. That's what towboats did on the Big Muddy. He'd yet to see any vessel *towing* another on the Missouri-Mississippi-Ohio system. While more savvy with the ways of a rope with a cow on the other end, he assumed the tricky currents and sudden surprises of the inland waterways made watermen proddy about pulling anything after them on the end of a slack line. So-called towboats were cinched tight as ticks to the bigger vessels they really pushed, as if they were a sternward extension of them.

The beer the old cuss had brought him was ice cold as well as brewed Dutch-style, the way they made it down by Saint Lou since all them squareheads had come West. But as he worked his way down the schooner he decided he was wasting time there. He shoved the almost-finished drink aside and lit a cheroot to give himself some time as he pondered his next move.

It was simply too early on a working day to pick up any riverside gossip, and if he waited until later it might be too late. He needed a powwow with someone who knew this stretch of river better than he did. He'd already considered and dismissed the newspaper morgue he'd used so well the last time Billy Vail had sent him over this way to foil that big robbery out at the fair grounds. A certain female reporter had made pretty good use of *him* too, and right now he needed information about Lucky Lovelace way more than he needed another roll in the hay with a lusty busty blonde— albeit come to study on it, that crazy little blonde and the sultry Aura Lee taking turns with him sounded . . . Sort of dangerous, come to study on it twice.

He put a nickel by the almost-empty glass, outrageous as such a tip might be, and made ready to rise and go forth in search of the truth when the old geezer came back out with another schooner of beer. He told Longarm, "I see you're about done with the first one. Spike, the barkeep inside, says he'll bet you're a sporting gent, asking about steamboats on account you've money riding on the unofficious race betwixt the *Morning Star* and the *Prairie Rose*."

"I've only heard a few words about it," Longarm replied, truthfully enough. "Seems to me I heard steamboat races have been outlawed on interstate waterways since some asshole blew himself and all his passengers clean out of the river with his safety valve wired shut."

The old-timer nodded, but said, "I just told you they was doing it unofficious. Laws passed by landlubbers in Washington is one thing, and the natural customs of the Western waterman are another thing entire. The two lines have been competing ferocious for the little first-class passenger service left since the infernal iron horse come puffing over the horizon after the war. I hear tell there's a mail contract at stake too."

Longarm frowned thoughtfully and said, "I, ah, heard the folk who ran the *Minnitipi* up as far as anyone can had the U.S. mails all to themselves these days."

The old-timer put down the fresh suds, scooped up the empty as well as the nickel, and confided, "Captain Gloria Grimes bought the *Morning Star* off another outfit on the Ohio when they went bust trying to compete with railroads. If you know of Captain Gloria and her pilot, Jim Truman, you know who figures to win, albeit some do say the *Prairie Rose* has the edge, drawing a foot less water. She was made for the Western rivers, you see."

Longarm saw something else. But Billy Vail hadn't sent him all this way to find out if that pretty little Widow Grimes had ever gotten things straight with her handsome but awesomely shy pilot yet. He said, "Knowing Gloria Grimes, I don't find it odd she'd race all comers across a freshly watered lawn before she'd let another outfit horn in on her upriver service. Who runs the *Prairie Rose,* and more important, which one's the most luxurious as to passenger accommodations?"

The old-timer thought, a good sign, before he decided. "I'd pick the *Prairie Rose* if I was picking fancy frills. She's newer, with a bigger boiler and sternwheel. Draws a foot less water, like I said before. I still got my money on the *Morning Star*. Miss Gloria's been giving good service since her husband got kilt a spell back, and old Jim Truman knows every bend of the river as far up as the mud's at all wet."

Longarm said that still hadn't told him much about the competition. The old-timer shrugged. "Bigger outfit, run by an infernal board of directions instead of watermen you can size up one damn way or the other. They bought out the old owners and spruced her up to run fast and shallow, hoping to beat out everyone else come low water or high. Her wheel is broader and digs in less'n the wheel of the *Morning Star*. She draws no more'n twenty-four inches even though she's a floating palace next to the poor little *Morning Star*."

Longarm sighed. "I'm commencing to get the picture. Is it safe to bet that no matter who wins in the end the flashy sports will be most likely to bet on the *Prairie Rose*?"

The old-timer nodded. "Riding on her too. Like I said, a floating palace, and Captain Gloria don't allow no serious whoring or gambling aboard her own mail packet. Are you aiming to drink that damn beer or did you just come down by the river to chew my poor ear?"

Longarm produced another nickel and said, "I can only drink so much at a time, this early, but I'd be proud to buy *you* one, if you'd like to wet your whistle along with mine."

The old man scooped up the coin and said he'd drink his inside. But at least he stayed put as Longarm managed to question him further about the sporting event neither the newspapers nor indeed the law was supposed to know too much about.

The old-timer said the *Morning Star* would be shoving off from Omaha as usual, in mid-afternoon with some mail from the East. The rival *Prairie Rose* had announced the same departure time from Council Bluffs, across the way. That gave Lucky Lovelace yet another reason to board the newer sternwheeler, if he meant to board either.

It seemed a shame as well as likely. For if little Gloria hadn't married up with Jim Truman after all . . . But what the hell, Billy Vail had sent him to arrest a killer, not to get laid, blast his unromantic hide. The notion of pretty little Gloria Grimes having a two-faced killer hiding out amid her passengers didn't set well with Longarm in any case. He'd have enough on his plate if the son of a bitch was aboard the rival *Prairie Rose*.

Somewhere in the distance someone was playing tinny music with more enthusiasm than skill. The tune was "Rally round the Flag" or "The Girl I Left behind Me," depending on which keys the distant organ player was hitting by mistake. Longarm could make out the rising cotton balls of the steam calliope now, between two more serious plumes of coal smoke as the sidewheeler with all this noise and smoke moved closer. The old-timer across from Longarm perked up to sing along:

> I belong in the Infantry
> And don't you think I oughta?
> We're marching down to Richmond Town.
> To give the foe no quarta!

39

Longarm said, "I'd have gone with 'Rally round the Flag.' I take it that's a showboat heading Lord knows where despite her six-foot draft, at least?"

The man more familiar with the Omaha riverfront opined, "You'd be right about her being a showboat. Wrong about her drawing that much water. She'd be *Captain Fagan's Floating Follies* outten Cairo, Illinois. Fagan bought that big slab of wedding cake off a New Orleans-to-Memphis line as used to run her deep-drafted as you suggest with her cargo deck crammed with cotton and buffalo hides. With her cargo deck converted most entire to a set-down theater, she don't draw more'n three full feet with no audience aboard. Captain Fagan ain't about to steam for one town with the folks from the last town still setting there, so—"

"I can see she's riding high for a sidewheeler," Longarm noted as the showboat swung broadside to them to proceed upstream, caliope blaring fit to bust. He could see she had *Miss Baton Rouge* emblazoned across her portside paddle box in once-gilt lettering. The fact she'd once been a passenger palace plying the lower Mississippi didn't worry him half as much as the news she was out of Cairo these days. He asked the old-timer if the noisy showboat accommodated passengers between landings.

The older man shrugged and said, "Doubt it. For openers she'd be crowded, topside, despite her cavernsome converted cargo deck. Fagan puts on variety acts as well as a new play ever' season. They carry a heap of actors, singers, ladies as don't mind being sawed in half, and all."

Longarm went on staring thoughtfully at the midstream sidewheeler as he mused, half to himself, "I've tagged along with touring actors, opera singers, and a Wild West show in my time. They're often short of help. Largely on account of they're often short of cash to pay the help. Kids are always running away with such outfits, working for free in exchange for a chance to see the world, or avoid being seen by some of it."

The old-timer shrugged and said, "Well, any kids who've run away from you won't get far aboard *Captain Fagan's*

Floating Follies. They might make Sioux City by midnight, Lord willing and the river don't drop much more. Either the *Morning Star* or the *Prairie Rose* figures to beat her there, starting hours later, for Captain Fagan ain't out set no records for speed. It's showboat attendance records he'd be most interested in, see?"

Longarm saw more than that. He got to his feet so nobody could mistake his meaning as he snapped another coin on the tin table and said, "I'd best get cracking then. If I had my druthers I'd get up to Sioux City ahead of both that showboat and those racing steamboats shoving off this afternoon. I don't suppose you'd know how a man might go about that, eh?"

The older man looked sincerely puzzled and replied, "Not hardly. I just told you either the *Morning Star* or *Prairie Rose* ought to beat that showboat there. But there ain't nothing leaving betwixt now and the start of the race that could get you there ahead of all three. If there was, it'd be in the race. No offense but even a cuss in a cowboy hat ought to have been able to figure that out!"

Chapter 6

Longarm had. It had still been worth a try. Knowing what came next and figuring he had the time to kill, he stopped at a barbershop near his hotel to sissify his hair and mustache a mite. He wouldn't be crossing over to Council Bluffs dressed as cow. He knew from his own eye for suspicious characters that nothing looked more suspicious than prissy duds and casual grooming that just didn't go together.

As he waited his turn behind a copy of the *Police Gazette*, Longarm listened to the locals, and as he'd hoped, the pending race between the two steamboat lines was a topic no stranger had to bring up on his own. Most of the older experts on the subject seemed to be rooting for Captain Gloria and her popular pilot, Jim Truman. But while they wanted the pretty daughter of one famous steamboater and widow of another to win, they tended to sadly conclude that the newer and more powerful *Prairie Rose,* piloted by the generally detested Turk Mason, had the edge.

When Longarm cautiously asked the balding local next to him how come they didn't care for this Mason gent, the local snorted in disgust and said, "To begin with, Turk Mason ain't no gent. He'd push his own mother into the churning paddles if he suspected it might offer him a cat's whisker less draft."

Another older man waiting to get his white whisps trimmed laughed and chimed in with, "Turk never had no mother. The devil jerked off on snake shit and the sun hatched him out! He don't just race. They all race, even if it is against the law. Turk races dirty, and don't even seem to care if he sinks his own passengers in the process."

The first, who seemed to know, nodded and said, "I'd never ride with that crazy son of a bitch. Captain Gloria's *Morning Star* will take you as far upstream as fast as the Good Lord wants a body to go. I've heard tales of pork lard in the firebox and safety valves wired shut."

Longarm cocked a brow and said, "That's not only illegal, it's an easy violation for the steamboat inspectors to spot."

There came a chorus of snickers, even from the one old barber. The white-haired customer explained, "Nobody could run a steamboat line without greasing the inspectors as well as the firebox coal. Not since speed's become so important on the very few river runs left."

The balding one nodded and said, "The slowest milk train has the swiftest steamboat beat all hollow, and leave us not forget all the twists and turns of the river next to tracks laid out by drunks. Win or lose, poor little Gloria Grimes will be lucky if she holds on to her mail contract another few years. That's what the sons of bitches backing Turk Mason and the *Prairie Rose* are after, the mail contract up above Milk River, where mail trains don't go yet."

Longarm almost gave away his own knowledge of that mail contract, since he'd saved Gloria Grimes from losing it a spell back. But he'd started the conversation in hopes of getting more information, not to give any out free. So he resisted the urge to ask why even greedy steamboaters would be out to grab a dying business from a marginal survivor of the prewar shining times of the steamboat trade.

Longarm mildly inquired as to how a steamboat skipper with such a rep could get any steamboat company to hire him. It was generally agreed the Wall Street dudes who funded such enterprises were total assholes who neither knew nor cared the way things were done west of, say, the

Hudson River. One old-timer sporting careworn Spanish spurs on his expensive but scuffed border boots laughed and said, "That ain't the half of it. I just solt ten thousand head of Gulf Coast cows to a beef syndicate based in Glasgow, Scotland, as just went into business over in the Nebraska sandhill range without ever laying eyes on neither a blade of U.S. grass or a hair on a U.S. cow. They calls such sneaky ways of doing business investigation. Ain't that a bitch?"

Longarm couldn't help saying, "I think you mean investing, but I agree it's a bitch. Common sense tells you men on the spot tending the chores ought to be able to beat the moneybags back East at the art of showing a profit from one's honest or, hell, dishonest efforts. But somehow, things don't always work that way."

His true but cynical observation inspired the white-haired cuss to ask personal questions Longarm didn't want to answer. So he shut up and waited his turn. The barber was fast. He had to be to pay his awesome rent on Leavenworth Street, most likely. Nonetheless, it seemed forever before Longarm was once more on his way, half scalped and reeking of bay rum and Macassar oil, knowing more than he'd been really interested in about business opportunities upstream from Omaha this summer. He checked his watch as he strode through the lobby of his hotel. It wasn't as bad as he'd feared. He still had plenty of time to change and get on across to Council Bluffs if he kept his last farewells to Aura Lee short and sweet. Thanks to all those boring old farts at the barbershop, he felt pretty sure he could pass for an adventurous businessman scouting the opportunities opening up along the upper Missouri, now that both the buffalo and buffalo-hunting Indians had been reduced to more modest proportions.

Up in the room he'd hired next to Aura Lee's, he debated saying nothing at all to the gal on the far side of that thin door between their adjoining bedrooms as he shucked his duds, tossing each item across his made-up and as-yet-untested bedstead. He'd helped the warm-natured bounty huntress test her own bedstead pretty good just a short spell back,

44

and there was no telling who a man might meet aboard a steamboat that afternoon, all gussied up in fresh duds and smelling like a poet.

He decided to take life as it came, neither knocking on that tempting door nor refusing to answer if she heard him in here and knocked on the far side. As he tossed his gun rig aside and sat on his bed naked from the waist up, to haul off his boots, he heard bedsprings creak on the far side of the thin paneling. As a matter of fact Aura Lee's bed, next door, seemed to be creaking fit to bust if one assumed she was alone in there.

Longarm let his boots thunk loud as they might want to on the rug as he got 'em off, stood up again, and hauled down his tweed pants and cotton underdrawers. If she'd heard, or if they'd heard, next door, it hadn't inspired any halt to whatever in thunder might be going on. So naked as a jay but curious as a cat, Longarm moved over to the door, dropped to one bare knee, and put one gray eye to the keyhole.

Then it was all he could do to keep from laughing like a jackass. For he was staring smack at a sight he felt certain no man had been meant to stare at by the mighty excited gal alone on the bed next door. He could only see a little of her from this awkward vantage point, but what he saw was enough to tell him she'd found the morning a heap longer than he had. Her black skirts were up around her belly button, and she had one high-button shoe braced against each bottom bedpost, with her thighs spread and her privates exposed to the morning sunlight through the lace window curtains. She was surely strumming her old banjo as she moved her bare bottom with hungry enthusiasm, softly moaning like a lonesome little alley cat in heat.

Longarm muttered, "Fun is fun, but how could she be *that* frustrated after all the honest effort I put into her just this morning?"

He noticed his own virile member had been inspired to new heights as he got back to his feet. He smiled wryly and muttered, "Down, boy. We got us a steamboat to catch, and she has her own situation well in hand."

Then he considered how he'd feel if everyone he met for the rest of the day turned out ugly, or worse yet, pretty but too prim. So seeing as it was only right for a gent to take formal leave of a lady, and seeing that that lady was a friend in need, Longarm tried the brass knob and, finding the door unlatched, simply strode on through and followed his raging erection over to the gal jerking off on the bed, saying soothingly, "Hold the thought and let me in there to finish right for the both of us, little darling!"

Then he noticed the younger gal jerking off in Aura Lee's room wasn't Aura Lee at all. But she didn't seem to care, or even open her eyes to see who he might be as she moaned, "Yesss! Yesss! Don't tease me! Take me! Ravage me as I've never been ravaged before!"

So he did. Most men would have. And whether she'd been ravaged in her black poplin maid's uniform by a naked stranger before, or only dreamt she would be, she sure took her ravaging like a sport, until she came at least. Poor Longarm was still trying to get there himself when she suddenly seemed to become aware of where she was and what she was doing, with whoever he might be, and demanded, "Oh, good sir! What is the meaning of this? This room is supposed to be empty and, my Gawd, is that what I think it is inside of me? I'll have you know I'm a good Christian girl who's been saving herself for the man of her dreams!"

Longarm kept moving in her, it would have hurt like hell to stop, as he groaned, "What your dreams don't know won't hurt 'em, and I'm trying to break you of unhealthy habits, ma'am. I take it Miss Aura Lee checked out and you'd be the chambermaid?"

The younger and more boyishly built brunette raised her bare knees to hug him higher up as she closed her eyes again to answer, "Miss Lee's been gone for hours. Some gentleman came calling for her and they left together in his carriage. What was that about unhealthy habits? I only came in here to straighten up and . . . ooh, I felt that! And just as I was getting hot again too, you mean thing!"

He left it in her as he proceeded to unbutton her bodice, saying soothingly, "I ain't half done, if you ain't. But let's get you out of this uniform less you get it all rumpled, hear?"

She said proper ladies never got all the way naked in mixed company but that he had a point about her need to keep her uniform neat. So in the end she helped, and he found it worth the extra time and effort, once he noticed how becomingly she blushed, all over, when she caught a glimpse of herself in the mirror across the room.

She giggled and confided, "Land's sake, we look like a dirty French postcard, only dirtier. By the way, my name is Frannie and does this mean we're engaged?"

He assured her that ordinarily it might, but that he had to catch a sternwheeler up the river that afternoon and couldn't rightly say when or if he'd ever be back.

He was set for some waterworks, but she took it well, and also took it dog-style, confiding that she had an understanding with a neighbor boy back home in Cass County, a day's ride south. When she added they'd best hurry if they meant to come one more time before the housekeeper came looking for her, Longarm felt better about what he might have gotten his fool self into. Since Frannie seemed more experienced than she liked to let on, he finished right in her with her high buttons locked around the nape of his neck and her sassy bare behind off the edge of the bed so he could grind counterclockwise to her with his feet planted wide on the rug. She said she'd never taken it that deep, even with the boy next door or the hired hand who'd broken her in somewhat earlier. Then she said they were likely to get her fired if they didn't cut it out for now. So Longarm rolled off and questioned her some more about Aura Lee as he watched her dress and tidy up her hair with a skill that hinted at some practice.

Frannie couldn't tell him anything more than she already had. He knew the room clerk, downstairs, would have to have seen and heard more. So he kissed the sporting chambermaid a fond farewell and ducked back to his own room to get cracking while Frannie tidied up after them all in the sudden vacancy.

47

He'd gotten a mite sweaty again, bless her, but after checking the time and noticing how much pleasant time he'd had to bless her for, he contented himself with a quick dip. Then he hauled out his baggage and, starting with clean but still sensible underwear, proceeded to transfer himself into a cross between an Eastern dude and a riverboat gambler.

Money being no object to Billy Vail, as long at it wasn't *his* money, the old sneak had even sprung for a smaller and sneakier sixgun to wear in a prissy shoulder holster under the tailored frock coat. It was a double-action .45 Webley Bulldog, a British handgun made for the Royal Irish Constabulary. Nobody had ever explained what George Armstrong Custer had been doing with a brace of such stubby weapons, rapid-fire though they were, at Little Big Horn, but Billy had assured Longarm it was a good enough gun out to fifty yards, and it was true that Longarm's usual .44–40 fucked up the drape of his new frock coat ferociously.

The damned old cravat he had to wear in place of his utilitarian shoestring tie was a bitch to tie right, even in front of a mirror. But he managed, and tried not to laugh at himself when he put on the really dumb hat Billy had bought him. He had to admit, once he had it on, that at any distance he looked like a couple of other gents entire.

Packing his real weapon and duds in one gladstone, he went down to the lobby with his baggage, and the clerk behind the counter didn't laugh at him after all.

Longarm announced he had to go up the river a spell, couldn't say for sure when he'd be back, and bet the clerk a dollar they couldn't store his baggage for him till he did.

The clerk said the usual bet was five, good to the end of the month. Longarm grimaced and said, "I noticed you even got rugs in the halls upstairs. Five it is, with four bits extra if you'd like to tell me about Miss Aura Lee, who had the room next to mine, until just now."

The clerk casually pocketed the six coins Longarm had spread between them as he said, "There's not that much to tell, since you already seem to know the lady's name and room number."

Longarm picked up his baggage and placed it atop the

marble counter as he growled, "That wasn't worth four bits, pilgrim."

The clerk moved the baggage down behind the counter for now as he replied, "It was your grand notion to offer. I'd tell anyone who asked that the lady just checked out. She said something about having to catch an earlier train than she'd planned on. The gent who came to fetch her must have shown up earlier than expected."

Longarm said, "I hadn't heard she was expecting anyone but me for, ah, lunch. Did this unexpected visitor have a name?"

The clerk nodded and said, "He did. Paul Henderson. I didn't have to make a note of that because Mister Henderson stays here when he's in Omaha. Your Miss Lee seemed surprised to see him when they met in the lobby, oh, an hour ago, I guess."

Longarm frowned thoughtfully and said, "As well she might have. She told me she was searching for a Paul Henderson and then some! You say they went off together, both willing, as far as you could tell?"

The clerk nodded and said, "In Mister Henderson's own carriage, as a matter of fact. Are you suggesting a guest of this hotel might have been . . . good heavens, what?"

Longarm pursed his lips and replied, "Ain't sure. I'd best 'fess up and tell you both me and Miss Aura Lee pack badges, official and private. She had a warrant on a jasper called Paul Henderson. So think harder."

The clerk did and decided, "Everything seemed friendly enough to me from where I stand this moment. Miss Lee did express some surprise at meeting Mister Henderson yonder, by that rubber plant next to the plush sofa. He said, let me see, something about hoping she might be here and that they had a lot to talk about. She seemed to agree to that indeed. Then they went up to get her things, she told me she was on her way to catch a train, and now you know about as much as I do."

Longarm muttered, "That ain't much, is it? Might there be a train bound for El Paso, leaving Omaha earlier than the usual one this evening?"

49

The clerk nodded and said, "As a matter of fact, you could still catch the El Paso Early Bird if you ran for it right now!"

Longarm asked, "What about the Sioux City steamer, *Prairie Rose*? Would it be possible for me to make the U.P. depot, then scoot across the river to Council Bluffs, in time to, ah, see friends off at both places?"

The clerk looked amused and said, "You sure have a lot of friends. If I were you I'd make up my mind *muy* damned pronto whether I wanted to wave *adios* to the train on this side of the river or the steamer on the other. There's just no way you'd ever manage to do both."

Chapter 7

Since he was damned if he did and damned if he didn't, Longarm did what he'd been told to do. He was hoping for a Western Union office within sight of the boat landing the *Prairie Rose* was about to shove off from. There wasn't any. There'd be no way to wire Denver till the wedding cake he was about to board made it up the river to her next scheduled stop at Sioux City.

Oily black smoke was rising impatiently from the forward funnels of the sternwheeler, and he could see they'd about finished loading. Whipping out his notebook and a stub pencil, Longarm paused by a big crate to scribble a terse message to his home office. Then he waved a curious colored workman over and said, "I have to board that Sioux City steamer before she shoves off. Is there a Western Union anywhere around here and would you like to make an honest dollar?"

The gentleman of color said he surely would, as long as it was honest. Longarm handed him the message and a silver cartwheel, saying, "You only have to hand this note to the telegraph clerk. It's official government business, to be sent collect."

The somewhat older but possibly uneducated workman looked confused. Longarm assured him, "You don't have to understand. You just have to put the dollar in your pants and put the message on the counter at the Western Union. It's all written down. They'll know what to do. Do we have us a deal?"

The bemused African-American grinned and said he'd see Western Union got the note and that what happened after that was up to white folks. So Longarm put his notebook away and legged it on for the gangway of the *Prairie Rose*.

As he boarded, he looked about in vain for any sign of the other steamboat his old pals, Gloria and Jim, would be taking upstream this afternoon, if that barbershop gossip had meant toad squat.

He didn't see anything half as impressive as the *Prairie Rose* tied up or out on the river right now. Despite her freshly painted gingerbread, the *Prairie Rose* was laid out much the same as any such craft had to be on the upper Missouri.

From, say, Saint Lou to the Mississippi Delta, one could count on between nine to twelve feet of water to push your flat hull across. As one steamed further up the Big Muddy, however, the water got ever shallower as well as ever thicker. The Missouri sternwheeler was designed to dip her broad paddles no more than a few inches below the surface, and carry thirty or more cabin passengers and at least two hundred tons of freight through waist-deep water, if the Big Muddy was running friendly.

In a pinch steamers built for the upriver trade could claw their way across sandbars barely awash. To do so they were overpowered for their size with what amounted to a team of locomotive boilers port and starboard, about even with the wheelhouse atop the Texas deck, with their twin funnels rising forward and steam lines running aft to the engine room, where steam cylinders far bigger than any rail locomotive needed were required to crank the broad and massive paddle wheels. The apparently awkward sprawl of steam fittings and machinery served to keep the flat hull trimmed fore and after of its center of balance. The hollow core of the cargo deck was reserved for cargo, light or heavy, where it was least likely to throw the whole shebang any way its crew didn't want it to lean.

Sternwheelers plying fickle waters slid their bluff bows onto gently sloping landings rather than the vertical docks one might see in ports where the depth was more predictable from day to day or indeed from moment to moment. So the passenger gangway led up to the all-purpose maw of the bottom cargo deck. A flight of steps to either side led up to the cabin or passenger deck. As Longarm made for the starboard stairs he noticed that the *Prairie Rose* didn't seem to be carrying much freight back there in the tunnel-like gloom. There was still room for thrice the kegs and crates he could make out from the sunlit foredeck. Before he could see what might be up on the cabin deck a burly cuss wearing a beard, a purser's cap, and a cargo hook stepped between him and the stairway to inform him politely but with a hard-eyed stare, "All ashore as going ashore, mister. We're about to shove off."

Longarm nodded and said, "So am I. I'm sure I got the fare as far as Great Falls if you'd like to tell me what you're charging."

The purser shook his head and insisted, "You'd best scout up another steamer. All cabins are booked and all the place settings for supper are took. You might try the *Morning Star* over to Sloane's Landing. I hear they're anxious for more business and passage will run you a mite less, *Morning Star* having less to offer."

Longarm tried, "I'd never make it. They just told me both boats were fixing to shove off any minute. What say you carry me up as far as Sioux City? If you beat the *Morning Star* that far I'll be able to switch to her, right?"

The purser scowled and said, "We'll beat her. But you still got to haul it ashore, mister. We don't carry deck passengers on this high-toned run, and like I said, we ain't got room for anyone I ain't got on my passenger list for reserved space."

High above them a tinny whistle repeated the invite for anyone who wasn't coming to get the hell off. The purser said, "That means you. I'm trying to be neighborly, mister. But when I orders an all-ashore I expect to see little froggies hopping off my lily pad, pronto."

53

Longarm sighed and said, "I can see how all this might be leading us intelligent-looking gents into a dumb situation. I used to jump when others hollered froggy in a voice of command. But I got out of the army years ago and, like I said, I mean to enjoy me a steamboat ride at least as far upstream as Sioux City."

The purser said, quietly, "No shit, now, we're fixing to haul in the gangway and you wouldn't want to get that swell suit all wet and muddy, would you?"

Longarm shook his head and replied, "I don't intend to. I've told you I'm willing to pay for first-class passage, with or without a cabin or, hell, an easy chair to set in as far as Sioux City. You might not guess it, to look at this outfit I got on right now, but you'd still find it a heap more trouble to put me off at this late date than you might to just show me a place I can set and then leave me be."

The purser didn't seem convinced. He whistled as if to a dog. Two deckhands came forward, staring uncertainly at Longarm as the purser said, "This gent's going ashore now, boys. If he won't go ashore on his own two feet, you'd best toss him headfirst in that general direction, hear?"

The bigger of the two deckhands smiled pleasantly enough and told Longarm, "I'm sure you'd rather disembark sensible, right?"

Longarm smiled back and said, "Hold on, boys. This is rapidly drifting from testy to unlawful. This infernal sternwheeler is a vessel chartered to furnish public transportation on the inland waters of these United States."

The three of them exchanged amused glances. Longarm continued. "I am the public. I want some transportation and I've offered to pay my damned way. You might or might not be able to refuse me my just rights to steam up the river to Sioux City like any other American citizen. If I survive the fight I mean to take the matter up with the interstate commerce division, Department of the Interior."

"Throw the silly bastard overboard," the purser decided, and they might have tried, had not another gent with "Captain" emblazoned in gilt thread above the leather bill of his cap come forth from the shadows to announce, "Belay that

54

notion, Mister Sweeny. I'll deal with this. You boys haul in and cast off whilst I explain the situation to Marshal Long here."

The purser stared thundergasted for a moment, and then he chased the deckhands forward to carry out the skipper's orders. Longarm sighed at the older and shrewder-looking pain in the ass to say, "I'd only be a deputy marshal, and I sure wish we could keep our own little secrets, Captain—ah . . . ?"

"Gilchrist, Jacob Gilchrist, and I remembered you from the time you took out some river pirates for the Postmaster General. Up near Kimaho, wasn't it?"

Longarm nodded and grudgingly replied, "Close enough," glad to see Gilchrist didn't seem to know about that other case in detail. It stood to reason others up and down the Big Muddy would have heard a few garbled details of a complicated case he didn't want to get into right now. He said, "I'm not worried about the U.S. mails or anyone running anything else up and down the river now. They sent me to bring in a killer known best to Uncle Sam as Lucky Lovelace. Your turn."

Gilchrist blinked in surprise, figured out what Longarm meant, and said, "We've nobody called Lovelace or even Lucky on our passenger list, if that's what you mean. What does your suspect look like?"

The deck was throbbing under them now as Longarm replied, "He ain't no suspect. We *know* he's killed at least two federal employees. But we don't know what he looks like. That's how come I was trying to board this tub discreetly and mingle with your passengers in hopes he'd give himself away. I don't suppose there's any way to keep my true identity a secret topside now that you've recognized me?"

Gilchrist smiled boyishly. "Sure there is. I'll just tell my boys not to tell any of the passengers. Sweeny was telling you true about our running a mite crowded this trip. We can't offer you a cabin, but if you think you'll be able to expose this Lovelace cuss betwixt here and Sioux City, you might not need one, right?"

They were backing off the landing now. The grating let up as the hull floated free, only to be replaced by a lower-pitched but more powerful throb as the paddles, out of sight but never out of mind no matter where one went aboard a sternwheeler, dug in for some serious travel.

Longarm said, "I might be able to spot the man I'm after, if I have your permit to start a friendly card game or two in your main salon."

Captain Gilchrist shrugged. "I'll show you up to the salon then. I doubt you'll have to start all that many card games, once the novelty wears off and it's dark outside. Card games have a way of starting themselves on riverboats. I wish I could say all of 'em are always friendly."

Chapter 8

Longarm and Captain Gilchrist parted friendly enough on the forward cabin deck. The skipper went on up to the wheelhouse to oversee their notorious pilot, Turk Mason. Longarm ducked into the forward salon for a drink to nurse. Though far smaller than one of the floating palaces the lower Mississippi was famous for, the *Prairie Rose* was still well appointed, with her salon much plusher than, as well as about the same size as, the Long Branch in Dodge. The bar along the back bulkhead looked like real mahogany. The barmaid's red hair was likely fake. But she served him genuine Maryland Rye with a chaser of Saint Lou lager, almost as tangy as the famous steamer beer they served out on the Sacramento Line frequented by gold miners and the fancy-dressed women gold miners could afford.

Save for the henna-rinsed barmaid, who looked like she teased more than she put out for tips, he spied no play-pretties of the female persuasion as he eased his way forward with his liquor glasses large and small. The salon wasn't halfway crowded yet, despite what the purser had said. His fellow riverboat passengers seemed a mixed lot, albeit nobody was dressed cheap. A couple of obvious Indian traders were dressed loud as hell, but neither they nor Buffalo Bill could have picked up all that snow-white deerskin and

57

Venetian glass beadwork for less than a month's pay doing anything honest.

Longarm sipped some beer, dropped the shotglass of rye in the rest of it, and strode out on the promenade with the tidy drink he'd made. He saw right off where everyone else had wound up. There was no place to sit or even lean along the port rail. It was a wonder they weren't listing with all those gents on that same side. Bracing his own broad back against the vertical planking of the cabin, he tallied the crowd at two dozen. Allowing for the half dozen he'd seen inside, and mayhap another handful jerking off in their cabins, the purser had been right about them having hired out all the cabins. There were usually six or seven cabins along each side deck, making bunks for around thirty, doubled up. That meant Lucky Lovelace was sharing a cabin with a stranger if he'd really lit out from Cairo alone. Knowing how he'd feel about that himself if he had anything on his mind that he might blurt out in his sleep, Longarm made a mental note to watch for passengers paying double to hog a cabin private. So far he hadn't spied a thing worth following up on. The deckhands he'd almost tangled with, below, looked as much like the man he was after as anyone else, until such time as he knew what the son of a bitch really looked like!

One of the others along the rail called out, "Here she comes and how come we ain't doing nothing about it?"

Longarm craned higher to peer over their infernal hats as, a mite further out and still a dozen boat lengths back, another sternwheeler came boiling up the river with a bone in its teeth under twin plumes of sulfurous smoke. Longarm didn't have to hear others groaning about female skippers being a crime against nature to know that had to be the *Morning Star,* Gloria Grimes commanding, with old Jim Truman at the helm.

Their new sternwheeler was somewhat larger as well as obviously more serious than the huffing and puffing *Minnitipi* he recalled so fondly from an earlier chase up the Big Muddy. He didn't have to be told why they were

58

burning coal this far downstream from the foothill forests. Cottonwood and willow gathered along the banks were good enough for casual steaming, but it took fuel solid as hickory or, better yet, coal to really boil water at the rate a big Corliss engine used it. Since either hardwood or coal had to be shipped out to the Western rivers these days, coal made more sense.

"They're passing us!" wailed a passenger. "What's wrong with old Turk Mason this afternoon? When's he gonna take his thumb outta his ass and open the throttles, damn it?"

Longarm knew. But he wasn't out to draw needless attention to himself. Another at the rail explained, in a less hysterical tone. "Turk knows what he's about. It's early and the water's a mite low despite the decent snowfall we had for a change last winter. The channel's deep enough right now. But the river commences to shoal in places up above Fort Calhoun. Once we pass the army post, you'll see one hell of a hairpin with the sandbars shifting even as you watch. A pilot guessing wrong about a slick or boil can wind up hard aground in the middle of the damned old river and then where's your bet?"

Another insisted, "Jim Truman's abeam and passing now, and they say he's one of the best on the river, come high water or low."

Longarm stared wistfully across the gap of muddy water between the two vessels as, sure enough, it grew wider again as the *Morning Star* took the lead. Longarm could make out the dark outlines of two small heads in the wheelhouse over yonder. He couldn't tell, from here, which head was piled with silky auburn hair a man wanted to run through bare-ass. The hell of it was, he never had. He'd had the chance, that time alone on the river with the lonely as well as lovely young widow. He'd passed on the one chance she and fate might have offered him, afraid of the way things might have turned out in the cold gray light of returning reason. He'd never forgiven himself. He often wondered if Gloria had. But Jim Truman had been as sweet on her, as well as a more sensible choice for a steamboating gal, so what the hell. And there was always that barmaid inside if a man got really desperate to rumple red hair.

"I see what Turk's up to," another passenger decided aloud as, up ahead, the *Morning Star* seemed to have horned in dead ahead of the *Prairie Rose*. Longarm didn't need to be told the unseen pilot above them had deliberately swung into the muddy wake of the famous pilot. The same sly passenger opined, "Turk knows they have a damned fine pilot as well as less power in a pinch. He means to let them show us the way, taking all the chances, till we're above the tricky channels and gloomy guesswork this side of moonrise. Then, come the full moon shining on the river and the clear run above the sandy delta of the Little Sioux . . ."

"Excuse my dust, *Miss Morning Star*!" said the one who'd been most worried, up to now, with a laugh.

Longarm drifted forward with the crowd, nursing what was left of his beer, this time to find his own place at the rail and see that, sure enough, the sternwheeler ahead had swung clear of a satin-smooth patch of the Big Muddy and that their own pilot had avoided the submerged snag as easily. Longarm felt sure Turk Mason would have spied the danger in broad-ass daylight even without another pilot to tag along after. Longarm hardly considered himself a steamboat man, and Gloria had shown him, that time on the upper river, how to spot a waterlogged tree on the bottom by the innocent patch of quieter water just downstream of the hidden hull-ripper. This far downstream the main channel was wide as well as deep enough to swing wide of anything at all suspicious. It would be further up, where there was much less river to work with, where a pilot might be forced to choose, suddenly, between the safer of two swirling slicks with nothing but the tumblewaters of new shoals anywhere else.

His beer schooner being empty now, Longarm went back inside to order another and find a seat at an end table.

There was more to admire along the east bank of the river than the ass end of another sternwheeler. They were well north of Council Bluffs now, albeit still in sight of the riverside rises that gave the town its name. Puffs of smoke were rising above the trees growing along the tops of the chalky bluffs. You couldn't make out the northbound train itself, but nothing else that threw up smoke like it moved half so sudden over land or sea. An older gent dressed like a sort of sissy buffalo hunter spied the locomotive plume about the same time, and demanded, as if Longarm had anything to do with it, "Say, is that a damned old railroad train racing up the river with us yonder?"

Longarm nodded, but said, "It ain't no race. That'd be the Burlington and Quincy day-tripper, and even stopping every few miles along the way she'll beat us to Sioux City by sundown."

The fancy dresser protested, "Captain Gilchrist says there's just no way we'll ever make Sioux City before sundown. We'll do well to pull in this side of midnight, ahead of that other steamboat."

Longarm nodded soberly and replied, "I just said that. A boat or barge can carry way more, way cheaper, but a train or, hell, a coach and six can get there faster. It's bad enough on still waters. Right now we're trying to go one way whilst the river under us is going the other. But don't get your bowels in an uproar, old son. We're traveling in comfort, and Sioux City can't be a hundred miles from here now, counting all the twists and turns."

The more anxious passenger grimaced and decided, "Just so's we beat the *Morning Star* up yonder. Which pool are you in, the one offering even money on each day's run or the one grand prize if we beat her to the landing at Milk River by a full day?"

Longarm confessed he'd come aboard at the last minute, as a traveler rather than a betting man.

The older gent pretending to be an overdressed frontiersman told him, "You'd best get cracking if you want to wager on this afternoon's run. I ain't sure you can now, seeing we're already under way with the *Morning Star* a dozen lengths out ahead of us."

"There's a heap of river left to run," Longarm pointed out in a desperately casual tone. "Who's running this pool you just mentioned, the purser?"

The older man shook his head and replied, "That wouldn't look right. Steamboats ain't supposed to race no more, official. How would it look if Norm Sweeny and Captain Gilchrist pulled a *Sultana* after accepting wagers off all of us?"

Longarm agreed that'd look awful. The sidewheeler *Sultana* had blown herself and a heap of passengers to kingdom come just after the war, resulting in worldwide headlines and much tougher regulations on the inland waters of these United States. The *Sultana*'s boiler explosion had not only been the biggest such disaster on record, but the result of stupidity across state lines. The federal government had been trying ever since to regulate river traffic, with safety taking precedent over speed. The race going on right now showed what most rivermen thought of such sissy notions. But as long as nobody connected with either steamer line owned up out loud to racing for money, there wasn't much anyone could do about it, as long as both crews showed respect for the few navigational rules that both statute laws and established custom agreed on.

The passenger who seemed to know so much confided, "Silk Fitzroy is the man you want to see about buying your way into the pool. I fail to see him about right now. He's likely in his cabin, going over his notebooks. I'll tell him you want in, soon as I see him, Mister—ah . . . ?"

"Call me Brazo, last name's Long," said Longarm, truthfully enough when one considered his Mex pals really called him Brazo Largo, or Longarm, in Spanish. He had to give his real last name, however fast, lest that captain make a fibber out of him with a slip or a broken promise. The older man in the fringed white deerskins didn't seem to get excited one way or the other. He said he was a Major Wellington, C.S.A., and that he was interested in the northern herd now that most of the buff down along the Staked Plains had been shot off.

Longarm thought about giving him a rundown on those buffalo still left north of the transcontinental rails. But on reflection nobody had asked him, and Billy Vail hadn't sent him to hunt buffalo. He stretched the truth a mite by saying,

"I might have heard mention of a gambling man called Silk Fitzroy. We are talking of a soft-spoken gent of average appearance but expensive tastes, right?"

Wellington shrugged and said, "That sounds as much like old Silk as it does anyone else aboard. Some fault him for his silk cravat and fancy French toilet water. But old Silk enjoys a rep for playing fair and paying when he loses."

Longarm tried not to sound sardonic as he asked if the gent taking wagers on the outcome of this day's run lost all that often. Wellington laughed easily and replied, "Nope. He'd be a piss-poor gambler if he made a habit of losing. But like I said, Silk wins fair, as far as any of us have ever been able to tell."

"You've known him a good spell then?" asked Longarm.

To which the older man replied with just a hint of realization, "I just told you I'm new in these parts. When I say we, I mean all us sporting businessmen in general. More than one old boy I've met afore down Texas way has assured me the pool aboard this tub's being run by a long-established professional, like I just said."

Longarm reached for his smokes to give himself time to think before he had to answer that.

Wellington looked sort of pouty for a man his age, and insisted, "Silk Fitzroy is all right. Do I look like the sort of asshole who'd bet serious money with a stranger he didn't know nothing about?"

Longarm offered him a cheroot. Wellington took it, dubiously, and said he'd smoke it later. Longarm lit his own, not letting his annoyance show as he idly wondered whether the snooty old fart would pass the three-for-a-nickel smoke on to some crewman or just toss it over the side, the wasteful son of a bitch.

They talked some more. Then Wellington got up to go out on deck and see how they were doing. Longarm could see from where he sat, inside, that the blood-red sternwheel of the *Morning Star* was still churning muddy froth at them less than a furlong ahead.

As Longarm rose, the henna-rinsed barmaid across the room called out to him. He moved over to the bar. She repeated, "I was saying if you'd like another drink within the next hour or so, you'd best order it now, sir. I get me a cabin break in mid-afternoon. It's supposed to make up for keeping this bar till Lord only knows when after supper."

Longarm said he'd best order a pitcher of beer in that case, and as she poured one for him, he asked, or observed, "There's just no saying, at supper time, what time you get to knock off at Sioux City, right?"

She grimaced. "You know it. This bar closes at midnight, official. But there's money to be made in the festive air of a late-night landing, and I'm keeping this bar to make money, so . . ."

Longarm paid for the pitcher of beer and told her soothingly that an hour or so in a bunk would no doubt do wonders for her. She shot him an arch look, decided that no matter how he'd meant that it was too risky, and allowed she'd see him later.

He sat alone at a corner table, sipping suds long enough to feel the sincere need for a serious leak. So leaving the pitcher where it was for now, he ducked out a starboard exit and strode aft to where, sure enough, the usual accommodations ran athwart the rear bulkhead, facing the loudly splashing stern wheel. He ducked into the chamber marked "Gents" and pissed a few pints down the simple sanitary device provided for pissing on a steamboat, a hole in the tiled deck near an upright slab of slate. The sit-down crappers emptied the same way so everything got properly whipped down and under by the descending paddles. It might have resulted in a mighty sloppy shithouse if they'd built it to hang over the paddles coming *up*, further forward.

Shaking the dew from the lily and buttoning up again, Longarm strode forward, along the port rail this time. He wondered which cabin door on which side concealed the mysterious doings of the nondescript Silk Fitzroy. The cuss would no doubt appear at supper in his own good time. If he didn't, then what? It wasn't simply unconstitutional to arrest the wrong man. It could tip the right man that a lawman was aboard, with *him* in mind.

He wondered which cabin might be that of the barmaid, and how red her hair really was, and whether she was amusing herself right now the same way that hotel maid had earlier.

He knew because so many had told him that gals who served the general public as barmaids, chambermaids, librarians, and such had to watch who they fooled with if they didn't want to risk their positions. So after hours spent flirting with gents they dared not encourage further, they tended to wind up in lonely if ingenious positions. It sounded discouraging as hell.

He wondered if she'd go for it if he assured her he was a tumbleweed just passing through with a friendly dong and a discreet lip. He decided that might make him look more like an asshole than discreet. He had enough on his plate if Lucky Lovelace was aboard, by any name or description. There was just no way to keep an eye on all the male passengers while examining the hair roots of the only female he'd seen so far.

Up forward, he found only a handful of the others out on deck, watching the boat ahead just hang in there, puffing and splashing as if it had plenty of time and the river all to itself. Longarm figured most of the others had gone to their own cabins to rest up from all the excitement or mayhap dress for supper. It seemed the sort of crowd that was used to dressing special just to eat.

Longarm finally got around to lighting that cheroot he'd hauled out to just sort of chew a spell. He'd been trying to cut down on his smoking ever since tobacco prices had gotten so steep. As he lit up he could judge the speed of the breeze against his bare face a tad better. Unless they were bucking a head wind, and the ripples of the river said they weren't, they were moving a couple of throttle settings faster than he'd thought, out here in mid-channel. He'd grown used to watching closer scenery receding faster from a train. Both vessels were steaming ten or twelve knots in relation to the surface, albeit more like a steady pony trot in relation to the banks as they had to buck the current. They were rounding a gentle bend right now. Longarm knew Jim

65

Truman, piloting the lead boat, was hugging the inside of the turn close where the slacker current ran without risking a grounding on the shallows the river built there by dropping silt as it slowed.

Up above, Turk Mason was trailing the *Morning Star* as if Truman were laying tracks instead of a wake. Longarm knew both Jim and the sometimes hot-tempered Gloria Grimes had to be aware of the bigger boat tagging behind them as if it were a tin can on a string. Longarm was tempted to wave. He didn't. He knew Gloria would never recognize him in this sissy outfit, and she could get sort of unpredictable when she felt someone was taunting her.

He tried to picture himself up forward, in the wheelhouse of the *Morning Star*. He'd been next to the sweet-natured but hot-tempered little steamboat gal as she'd steered the old *Minnitipi* through some slicks and boils no steamboat had any right to steam through still afloat. He knew Gloria and her own pilot knew this rival tub had about the same draft and a mite more power. He knew that given slack water and a clear channel he could likely beat Jim Truman in the home stretch himself. Blowing smoke out both nostrils, he murmured half aloud, "You're going to have to slicker us, honey. Unless you can lead us into sneaky waters, or unless you just don't give a hang, Turk and Captain Gilchrist are simply going to let you lead 'em not into temptation during the tricky parts of the run this side of moonrise, and then, along about that big bend above the Winnebago Agency, they'll just overtake and pass you on that last smooth run to Sioux City."

He went back in the salon to see if anyone had stolen his beer. Nobody had, and there were still signs of foam. He picked up a saltshaker to put a fresh head on it. It didn't change the taste, save for making it more salty if one over-did it. But beer was drunk on a lazy afternoon as much to kill time as for any other reason. Salting flat beer was no more disgusting than jacking off, when you studied on it.

Chapter 9

Supper aboard the prissy *Prairie Rose* was cooked and served French-style by colored help dressed up like hospital orderlies. The linen on the table was as spotless, and the pork chops even had on frilly paper garters for some reason.

Longarm saw he'd been right about some of the other passengers dressing even more fancy for supper. He saw, or had a pretty good notion, what at least some of them had been up to in their private cabins when he noticed more than one lady, or at least more than one female, digging in across from him. The big blonde flirting over the floral centerpiece at him wore real pearls as well as a phoney smile. The other play-pretties were gussied up expensively as well. That might have been why they felt obliged to talk at table, as if they were society ladies instead of what they likely were.

Longarm kept his mouth shut and his reservations to himself as he let others prattle on about steamboating on the upper reaches of the Big Muddy. Some asshole was holding forth on the existing record for a day's run above Saint Lou, held by *The Far West,* with Captain Grant Marsh. The dude was right about Grant Marsh averaging three hundred and fifty miles a day between July 3 and July 5, 1876. But he seemed unaware *The Far West* had been running downstream with wounded survivors of Little Big Horn.

Longarm figured a skipper good as old Grant Marsh might be willing to race as ferociously for serious money, but there was no way even he could move that sudden upstream, against the current.

As if to prove his unspoken point, the dull throbbing of the unseen paddles slowed just enough to make the brassy blonde across the way look startled and proclaim, "We're slowing down! I thought this was supposed to be a steamboat race!"

That inspired others to rise from the table without excusing themselves. As most of them chased the broad-assed worrier out on deck, Longarm helped himself to more sweet-pickle relish. As he did so he locked eyes with another experienced traveler who'd been seated next to the big blonde. Longarm smiled sheepishly and said, "These pork chops are handsome enough but a mite dry for my taste."

The other man, dressed even fancier with a linen napkin covering his watered silk cravat, ruffled shirtfront, and brocaded satin vest said, "Yep. With the gloaming light commencing to get tricky outside, both pilots will be less worried about speed than sawyers until the moon sheds more light on the subject."

Longarm spread some relish on his remaining pork chop as he nodded. "Moonrise'll be this side of nine-thirty, full and cloudless, if this morning's paper was any judge."

The stranger agreed that was about the way he'd read it and added, "They call me Silk, Silk Fitzroy. I don't believe I have your name written down anywhere yet, Mister . . . ?"

"Long, Brazo Long," Longarm replied with an innocent smile. As they shook across the relish he casually tossed in, "Someone told me you was the one covering the bets on this race."

Fitzroy laughed easily and replied, "Bite your tongue. There are state as well as federal rules forbidding commercial vessels to race on this river."

Longarm nodded, cutting up his pork chop as he observed, "Such navigating rules are almost impossible to enforce as long as nobody announces nothing, public. The same rules discouraging steamboat racing allow and even encourage P.D.Q. delivery of passengers and freight to their bought-and-paid-for destinations."

Fitzroy said, "You're learning. I don't work for either steamboat line, and there are no federal statutes at all in regard to the placing of wagers on most any uncertain event. It only stands to reason that two steamboats leaving Omaha about the same time are most unlikely to proceed upriver at the same speed, lawfully or not."

Longarm chewed and swallowed. It would have been rude to spit all that chawed pork out now, even if it was too overcooked to bother with. He washed it down with some of the icewater provided. "I just said the rules about steamboat races were impossible to enforce. As long as we're on the subject, does this pool I understand you're running provide various pots for various outcomes, depending on the odds?"

Fitzroy grimaced and said, "Within limits. I'm a professional gambler, not a professor of trigonometry."

Longarm looked sincerely interested. So the expensively dressed Fitzroy explained, "I've got my own money bet on certain outcomes, of course. But I cheerfully confess I don't have the personal cash to cover all bets by all comers. I'm running the pool pari-mutuel. You understand how that works, don't you?"

Longarm said, "Like a race track, with the winners paid off with the losers' money after you rake off a percentage for your own trouble. Can I ask how big a cut you figure you rate, Silk?"

Fitzroy smiled back just as friendly as he replied, "You can ask. That doesn't mean I have to tell you. Stage magicians never say how they perform their tricks either."

Longarm shrugged and stared about for their waiter. When he caught the haughty eye of the dusky gent and got him to come over, Longarm asked what was for dessert. He decided he'd try the Napoleon pastries. He'd had pie à la mode before, and this was the first he'd heard about Napoleon baking anything. As the waiter left to fetch his order, he turned back to Fitzroy and said, "Major Wellington said you enjoyed a rep for honesty. Tell me more about who wins what for betting how in this pool you're running."

Fitzroy relaxed a mite and explained. "There isn't enough bet on the *Morning Star* to make it worth just betting on this vessel to beat her to the end of the line. You can bet we beat her by an hour, two hours, three, and so forth. You can bet each port of call as it comes up, or you can bet the final outcome at the end of the line. In sum, you can wager on just how *Prairie Rose* will humiliate her rival along the way or at the end. The major you just mentioned placed an interesting wager with, so far, nobody covering it, should you feel lucky. He thinks we'll put in at Sioux City for as short a time as possible and then shove off again to get a good lead on *Morning Star* by moonlight. Why don't you bet both captains will leave Sioux City fair and square like sporting gentlemen?"

Longarm replied that whatever else she might be, Captain Grimes of the *Morning Star* was no gentleman. The waiter wheeled a whole tea table of fancy square cupcakes over. They were frosted chocolate, vanilla, orange, and other flavors a body could only guess at. Longarm was about to ask how in thunder they expected one man to eat that many of Napoleon's pastries when he remembered, just in time, that time he'd eaten at Delmonico's in the city of New York. He only took half a dozen, explaining to the worldly Fitzroy, "They show you all the kinds they got so you can choose a sensible portion." Then he said, "I'll pass on fancy figures anyone with half a mind might be tempted to fix. What do I win if I bet on the other boat beating this one to the end of the line?"

Fitzroy answered, flatly, "A lot. So far, only one other passenger has bet on Gloria Grimes and her *Morning Star*. So the two of you would split the whole pot."

Longarm let the waiter finish pouring him some coffee to wash down the Napoleons, and thanked him for both before he got around to asking Fitzroy who the other wild better might be. He wasn't surprised when the flashy dresser refused to tell him. Longarm said he understood riverboat ethics, but that he'd just keep his money in his pants for now, if it was all the same with all concerned.

Silk Fitzroy shrugged and allowed it was a free country. Longarm found the Napoleons a mite cloying, but the coffee was just right.

Silk Fitzroy didn't seem to want any dessert, or anymore of Longarm's company, for that matter. He said something about sundown as he left the table and strode out on deck. The other two passengers were too far down for handy conversation, and seemed to be playing footsies under the table, ugly as the woman was.

So Longarm polished off his own repast, lit an after-dinner smoke, and went out to the port promenade to discover the sun was sure enough setting ketchup-red behind the black-lace edging of treetops along the west bank. He seemed to have that side all to himself, despite the pretty scene. He headed around the stern to find out why. The paddles were thunking slow but steady, and now he could hear tin-whistle calliope music again. Someone was playing "Camptown Races" or "The William Tell Overture." In either case the good-natured sarcasm was self-evident. Longarm had to smile. He'd figured they'd catch up with that showboat well this side of Sioux City. But *Miss Baton Rouge* was moving even slower than he'd figured if she figured on getting there at all this evening.

As he passed between the male and female shithouses and the spray-boards of the sternwheel, Longarm encountered a colored deckhand coming the other way. There was room enough to pass each other without an argument, and Longarm would have let it go at that if he hadn't recognized the working stiff of color and demanded, "Hold on! Ain't you the one I paid good money to in vain, back in Council Bluffs?"

The burly deckhand didn't seem to be avoiding Longarm's eye as he innocently replied, "I sent that telly-gram for you, Cap'n."

Longarm asked, "How? They hauled the gangway in right after I come aboard."

But the deckhand replied, "I knows that, Captain. I

helped. I never said I run all the way my ownself. I gave your note to a young boy hanging about the landing, along with a whole dime to hurry him on his way, see?"

Longarm grimaced. "I've nothing against a man turning an honest profit. But how well might you know that kid you entrusted my message and mayhap a lady's life to?"

The deckhand looked away and sounded less sure of himself as he replied, "I've seen the boy along the Council Bluffs riverfront afore, Cap'n. Why would he let us down anyways?"

Longarm sighed. "For openers, it's way easier to go no place than it is to go anyplace, for the same fee, with nobody looking. Since there's no way to find out now, I can only hope the kid is dumb instead of lazy. I'm sorry I wasted your time and mine by trusting you back there."

The deckhand looked hurt. Longarm had wanted him to feel shitty. He was felling pretty shitty himself as he forged on around to the starboard promenade, knowing that if pretty little Aura Lee was in a jam she'd have to get out of it herself as best she could.

The reason all the other passengers seemed to be lined up along the rail facing east was self-evident to both the ear and eye. The big sidewheel showboat known as *Captain Fagan's Floating Follies* or *Miss Baton Rouge*, depending on whether one read her posters or paddle-wheel box, was puffing along abeam, her white gingerbread glowing more like orange cake frosting against the purple sky to the east as her own passengers, or Captain Fagan's theatrical troupe, waved back at the crowd aboard the *Prairie Rose*.

By craning a mite Longarm could see the *Morning Star* was leading the way just a few boat lengths ahead. Nobody was moving much faster in real distance than a man could have walked along the far bank. But since the river was rolling the other way, all three steamboats seemed to be moving upstream a mite faster, and even as he watched, Longarm saw the bigger showboat was starting to slowly fall astern, despite her gallant calliope music, or mayhap because her pilot knew what he was doing. The light was getting really tricky now, and just who was to say whether a dark dot swirling in the sunset-gilded current was just an old beer bottle on its way to New Orleans or the tip of a sixty-foot sawyer dragging its waterlogged roots along the bottom?

By the time he'd finished his cheroot and tossed the butt over the side to confuse or clarify things better, the light was getting even trickier and some of the others were drifting back inside. Longarm made a silent wish for Aura Lee on a bright star winking on against the deeper purple to the east, and ambled into the main salon himself.

The same henna-rinsed gal was back on duty behind the bar. She served him a wistful smile and another boiler-maker. As he turned from the bar again he saw that, as he'd hoped, a game of five card stud seemed to have started at a corner table. So he drifted that way, sizing up the six gents watching as well as the four seated at the table so far. The man who'd come aboard as Silk Fitzroy was dealing. This was no great surprise. An admitted professional who didn't want to play cards on a riverboat would have been the surprise. The slicker was dealing right-handed, meaning he wasn't really Lucky Lovelace, or meaning the wanted killer knew others knew about his usual habits if it was him. Wheels sure could spin within wheels when a wanted man showed a lick of common sense.

Longarm almost made the mistake of joining in. Just watching wasn't half as interesting, even though it was against Longarm's code to cheat when and if a game seemed on the level, as this one did, so far.

But Billy Vail hadn't sent him to play cards with Lucky Lovelace or anyone else, and he could study everyone better lounging casually and nursing a drink. He was glad he'd chosen that course of action when, on the far side of the salon, another game seemed to be starting up at another table. This time the dealer, a small shy individual Longarm had yet to talk to, was dealing five hands of rummy *left-handed*!

Longarm stayed where he was, for now, as if he were still most interested in the poker game. There was no law against being a natural southpaw. Close to one out of every ten folk were, whether guilty or innocent, and nothing had been said about the real Lucky Lovelace being a rat-faced shrimp. The federal wants on the killer complained he was nondescript in appearance. The southpaw dealing rummy yonder was outstandingly small and ugly.

Meanwhile there were heaps of other strangers aboard who might or might not deal with their right thumbs resting on the top of the damned deck. So when the so-called Major Wellington eased up beside him and asked if he'd like to help start another game, Longarm just had to decline with a wistful smile. There was no damned way a man sitting at one table could watch the hands of everyone playing cards all over the damn place—or even sitting in a corner flirting with the gals.

Knowing all the gals were taken, with the possible exception of that henna-rinsed barkeep, Longarm kept his mind on the other gents. The one thing Lucky Lovelace couldn't be disguised as was a sporting lady in a summer-weight bodice and better-than-average build. Some of the play-pretties along for the ride were a mite hard-eyed to Longarm's taste, but none of them looked tough enough to be a man of average size and appearance in disguise.

He still made a mental note to ask that purser, Sweeny, which of the men on board were traveling up the river with something more interesting than their own fists. That was if the infernal purser ever showed up again this side of Sioux City. The last reports on the infamous Lucky Lovelace had him traveling alone. So it was probably safe to eliminate any ordinary-looking left-handed dealers sharing quarters with a female, unless, of course, Lucky Lovelace *knew* they had him pegged as a lone wolf and so he'd picked up a pal this side of Cairo.

Longarm's vexation was showing as he went back to the bar for a second schooner of beer, this time without the rye. The henna-rinsed gal who tapped him another said, "Don't look so desperate, handsome. It ain't as if there's no hope for you. I just heard we won't be staying the night at Sioux City after all. We'll be pushing right on and, like I said, I get to shut down and toddle off to my own private quarters a little after midnight."

He cocked a brow at her and said, "Lucky for you. It so happens I don't have no cabin booked aboard this tub, Miss, ah . . . ?"

"My friends call me Billie. I know you come aboard too late to book your own cabin. That's how come I mentioned my own, unless you got something prettier lined up."

He told her, gallantly, "Miss Billie, there ain't nobody half as pretty as you aboard this boat," and neglected to add he meant nothing he had lined up leastways. For she wasn't bad, even if the alternative hadn't been dozing in a chair, sitting up, while everyone else got to lie down, at the very least.

But while the somewhat brazen little barkeep was commencing to look better to him already, the night was ridiculously young and he still had his duty to study on. So now that they seemed such pals, he casually asked her if most of the other gents paid cash, like him, or signed for their drinks to settle up with the purser at the end of the line. She confided, "I noticed earlier you were a decent tipper. That ain't why I mentioned the time I get off, though. I don't make friends that way. But I have found a gal can tell a lot about a man by the way he treats the help. I've never had much fun with either a stingy or a show-off man. Men who treat most everyone about right tend to treat most everyone about right, if you follow my drift."

He said he did, making a mental note she'd likely expect him to rock the man in the boat pretty good for her, and then he asked, as casually as he could, whether she'd noticed how many other passengers signed their bar tabs southpaw.

When she asked why he cared, with a puzzled frown, Longarm told her he'd just read one man in ten was left-handed and wondered if that was true.

Billie thought. "I'd say that sounds about right. I only notice when a customer signs awkward. Lots of southpaws sign with their hands above their signature instead of under, the way you're supposed to sign."

Longarm said, "I asked a southpaw about that one time.

She told me your hand drags through the ink on you if you hold the pen the way the rest of us do."

Billie wrinkled her pert nose and demanded, "And just what else did *she* do for you left-handed?"

Longarm laughed. "I can generally manage my own buttons. I was wondering about that little rat-faced cuss in the flat-topped hat and checked coat, corner to your right."

She shrugged. "That'd be Mister Webb from Saint Lou. He's a whiskey drummer and not a bad sort, far as I know. What about him?"

"Is he naturally left-handed, or only when he deals rummy?" Longarm asked.

Billie thought. "He does sign southpawed, now that you mention it. Is that supposed to mean something sinister?"

Longarm shook his head and assured her, "Not now. I reckon I must have had him mixed up with someone else I'd heard of."

She nodded. "You mean that killer you and other lawmen are searching high and low for along this old river, right?"

He sighed and didn't argue. He didn't ask who'd told her who he really was. It only stood to reason the whole crew knew by now. With luck, it might take the passengers longer, and all this time he'd thought Billie's invite was inspired by no more than his new suit and hair oil. He wondered if it bothered rich old men to be admired only for their money. He decided to screw her anyway, provided he couldn't figure out which one in the crowd was Lucky Lovelace before they made it all the way to Sioux City.

He knew that if the wanted killer did give himself away between now and, say, midnight, they'd both be getting off there and he wouldn't have to worry about whether this henna-rinsed sass was out to screw him just for fun or as company policy.

He smiled down at her and said they'd talk about it some more later on. As he drifted over to the rummy game he could see her reflected in a now-dark side window. She was smiling after him, sincere as hell. He didn't know whether he wanted to get off at Sioux City with an arrested killer or mayhap ride just another few hours up the Big Muddy and get off at Yankton or, hell, Chamberlain.

But he knew what Billy Vail would want him to do. So he decided to make a sincere effort and, if that didn't work, just take his beating from old Billie like a man.

Chapter 10

Card games sure were tedious when you weren't sitting in yourself. Longarm had lost track of the cheroots he'd smoked and the beers he'd drunk as he stepped out on deck to head back to the pisser some more. As he did, he saw the full moon was rising at last to the east, and sure enough the tempo of the thunking paddles was picking up again as the swirling darkness all around gave way to a moonlit surface running bright as candlelit quicksilver.

Letting his molars float just a spell, Longarm strode forward instead of aft, to see how his pals aboard the *Morning Star* might be reacting to all this light on the subject. He had to laugh when, as far upstream as he could see by moonlight, the *Morning Star* was nowhere to be seen!

As the deck tingled under him even more, he headed on back to let off some steam of his own, muttering, "Gloria and old Jim stole a march on you, Captain Gilchrist. I don't know why I just found it surprising that they opened up the other side of moonrise. I've ridden with Gloria Grimes before. She and her pilot know this river better than most, and even I might have speeded up on a straight, clear stretch of river, knowing the moon would be up before I could get in any real trouble, and knowing I had a pest sniffing along just behind me in the dark!"

As he entered the dark shittery, the paddles just a few yards away were going lickety-split and actually sucking air down the urinal slot. Longarm let fly a pint or more, muttering, "Kee-rist, they must be mad as wet hens up in the wheelhouse right now! The skipper's acting like he's got his own money riding on who gets to Sioux City first, as if there's any question about that now."

He buttoned up and stepped back out into the moonlit promenade, adding, "assholes," under his breath as somewhere below a gatling gun or mayhap a safety valve commenced to chatter. He was inclined to feel it had to be a safety valve. It was dumb to fire the boilers up to where you were popping your safety valves with more steam than your engine could use. But that was the whole point of safety valves when one studied on 'em.

In the days of flat-out riverboat racing, a skipper or two had blown himself and his passengers up by boiling water faster than any engine could ever use it. He'd read somewhere that one of the first horrendous steam explosions on record had resulted when a not-too-bright slave stoker, annoyed by the popping of a safety valve, had wired it shut. In the old days of unregulated river traffic, more than one sporting skipper had repeated that stunt, not out of sheer ignorance as much as because, if you figured the odds just right, a standard boiler with no steam escaping by way of its safety valve *did* offer more pressure, and hence more speed, than its built-in safety margin was designed for.

Up in the bows he could see others had come out on deck to marvel now. That was likely the end of the cardplaying this side of Sioux City. But what the hell, it wasn't as if he had to ride on sitting up, without a place to rest his weary head.

That was provided they made it all the way to Sioux City, or even around the next bend, at the rate they were going.

It wasn't their speed up the moonlit river that he was worried most about, albeit hitting a snag or sawyer going this fast was sure to open the bottom stem-to-stern. He found it much more ominous, as he moved up to join the others, that the safety valve he'd heard before wasn't popping now.

There were two ways to read that. The stokers could have noticed they were wasting coal and eased off. Or some maniac could have wired the valve shut in hopes of building more pressure and hence speed than their unseen rival further up the river could manage.

Longarm paused, amidships, muttering, "Hold on now. Was it the front end or the ass end where they said the bang was loudest? I think they said most steamboats blow up forwards. So how come we're headed up to the bow, you asshole?"

He was only half serious. But he did break stride and, in so doing, he threw the plans of another out of joint completely.

It was still bad enough. Longarm gasped, "What the hell . . . ?" as someone crashed into him from a suddenly opened gangway exit and the two of them reeled like waltzing roller skaters against the far rail.

There was no way to get at the gun in his shoulder holster without letting go of the son of a bitch he was tangled with, and since the son of a bitch seemed out to shove him over the rail, there was no way he was about to let go. So they went over the rail together.

Somewhere between leaving the cabin deck of the *Prairie Rose* and hitting the upper Missouri with a mighty splash, Longarm lost touch with his unknown assailant. But he was still sore as hell as he struggled back to the surface, coughing muddy water and dire warnings. Then he bumped asses with the hull of the sternwheeler he'd just parted company with, and not wanting to be pulled under by the sternwheel, shoved off with both boot heels and proceeded to swim like hell in hopes of clearing the plunging paddles!

He figured he had when he found himself spinning like a waterlogged ballerina in an eddy just astern of the rapidly receding *Prairie Rose*. As he saw he was clear of the damned paddles as well as either shoreline, in water over his head, he called out, "Hold on! Ahoy! Avast! Or whatever the hell it takes to stop a steamboat!"

But he knew nobody else knew he was bobbing down the damned old river, astern, with the possible exception of the prick who'd shoved him overboard. So he yelled, "All right, you prick, I was after you to begin with. So where are you and let's see if we can work our way to one damn bank or the other, hear?"

There was no answer. If that had been Lucky Lovelace, and he'd been pulled under by the paddles, he'd likely surface in three or four days, way closer to the Gulf, after he'd bloated enough to float.

Meanwhile, Longarm could only tread water till he had a better grasp of which bank might be closer. The winking stern lights and moonlit wake of the rapidly receding sternwheeler made her black boxy form way easier to follow with a wistful eye than even a catfish could have followed physically. She was over a furlong off now, as she suddenly turned into a mighty cotton ball of expanding white steam!

Longarm was smart enough to duck his head below the surface before the shock wave and flying debris caught up with him.

As he dove for the river bottom, desperately trying to get as much water between himself and all that showering sludge as possible, Longarm heard and felt ominous plunging splashes all around. He was far enough away, he hoped, to be out of range of really big chunks of flying steamboat. His blindly groping fingers dug into soft slimy mud. He tried to grip the bottom of the river to no avail. But he knew that even as he was running out of air, the current was sweeping him ever further from the big bang. So he let himself drift upwards till he bumped the bottom of something big and flat, floating on the surface amid all the lesser floating wreckage. As he hooked the soggy elbows of his no-longer-fancy frock coat over the splintery edge for a look-see all about, Longarm saw he'd lucked onto the roof of the wheelhouse. It was still in one piece after no doubt soaring skyward quite a ways on a rising column of steam. There was no mystery as to what must have happened to the rest of the wheelhouse, or the poor souls gathered about the wheel, when one or both boilers had gone off like a mighty barrel of gunpowder directly below them!

None of the others, gathered up in the bow, would have had much more of a chance. Those who hadn't been killed outright by the blast would have wished they had been by the time they drowned, too mangled and steam-scalded to swim worth mentioning. He still called out, more than once, in the unlikely chance someone besides his own fool self might still be alive out there on the swirling moonlit waters.

He got no answer as he hauled himself up on the raftlike floating roof. Taking quick stock, he found he'd lost that hat, but otherwise he still had both his sixgun and derringer, along with his wallet. First things coming first, he hauled off his boots to pour pints of muddy water out of 'em. He peeled off the soggy coat and laid that aside as well. Then, by the light of the prairie moon, he saw that while his personal identification and silver certificates were mighty soggy, the ink didn't figure to run too bad and the paper would dry, in time. His federal badge, of course, was even more waterproof than the wax Mex matches he packed along for wet weather, albeit hardly *this* wet, as a rule. He knew that if he hauled out a three-for-a-nickel cheroot right now it would be as easy to light and smoke as fresh cat shit. So he didn't try.

There was still the smell of hot oil and steam in the air. But anyone who hadn't just witnessed that horrendous shipping disaster might have never guessed there'd been one now. Longarm saw he seemed to be bobbing along on the biggest piece of wreckage afloat, and you always saw lots of shit floating down the river no matter what.

An eddy spun his perch around as if to afford him a 360-degree panoramic view of his soggy surroundings, and Longarm spied a handy length of planking. He laid hands on it, muttering, "Channel seems too deep to pole this particular raft, but we ought to be able to paddle one damn way or the other."

So he tried. Paddling a big rectangle of wood and canvas roofing in any particular direction would have been a bother with a regular paddle. Longarm found he did better after he dipped the splintered end in the water so he could grip the more neatly sawed end with the heel of a wet palm. He tried sitting astride one corner with his bare feet in the water as he paddled first to one side and then the other of the point he had aimed east. It seemed possible he was moving more to the east than west as the current carried him south faster. He was hoping for the east bank because that was the one the railroad ran along, leastways within walking distance. He knew the west shore of the Big Muddy, along this stretch, was much less settled. But after the current swirled him around in more than one complete circle, he was ready to settle for either damned bank. He told his improvised paddle, "This is ridiculous. I can feel you digging into the water, so how come you ain't taking me no place? I don't want to float all the infernal way to New Orleans."

Neither the paddling nor the bitching about it seemed to help. He seemed to be stuck out there forever at the mercy of the current as the Big Muddy swirled ever seaward.

Hardly forever, he decided with a weary curse. He knew that sooner or later the sun would rise again and that a man could hardly bob all the way down to New Orleans by broad daylight without somebody noticing and mayhap even doing something about it. He tried to console himself with that time the *Rocky Mountain News* had been carried off in the big Cherry Creek Flood of '63, editorial staff and all, and hadn't some cowhands finally roped the flagpole atop the roof from shore way downstream?

"They never lived it down and I ain't got that much time," Longarm decided, dying for a smoke.

Then he reflected that he might be getting his bowels in an uproar needlessly. Even if he floated all the way down to Omaha and beyond before he ever got ashore again, Billy Vail had wanted him out of town a spell, and as soon as one studied on it, he'd already accomplished his mission.

For if that hadn't been Lucky Lovelace who'd just saved his life by trying to kill him, and nobody else made as much sense, Lovelace would still be dead right now, whether scalded to death by that steam or chewed to chipped beef by those paddles.

"I still wish I had something dry enough to smoke," Longarm muttered as he bobbed along safe but bored shitless by the light of the silvery moon.

Chapter 11

Crawdad Cartier, pilot of the damnit *Miss Baton Rouge*, had enough on his plate as he peered upstream from his usually silent wheelhouse without worrying about whether that had been a distant thunderstorm they'd heard a spell back. At his side, puffing one of those goddamned old Havana Claro cigars, Captain Fagan of *Fagan's Floating Follies* repeated for perhaps the hundredth time, "The starry sky is still clear as a virgin's conscience, Crawdad. How do you account for thunder upstream when, as you can plainly see—"

"There's supposed to be silence on the bridge at all times when a steam vessel is underway!" the crusty pilot said, cutting in. "I told you before, it had to be thunder or a steamboat blowing up, dad blast it! In my time on this river I've heard both and they sounds a heap the same. I'm still hoping it was dry lightning. Searching for survivors is tedious, even by daylight. On the other hand, both them sternwheelers as passed us earlier were clawing upstream under more steam pressure than I'd want under *this* child!"

As if he'd been asked for his own opinion on such matters, their chief engineer, Curly Garth, entered the wheelhouse to report, "Got enough coal on the grates to last us to the next landing if you don't want to bust any records, Crawdad. What was that about survivors?"

The pilot swore softly and replied, "Regular lecture hall we seem to be running up here this evening. You likely missed it, down below amid the machinery, but half an hour or so back, as I was minding my own beeswax up here, something went bump in the night. The captain wants it to be something we can do something about. I'm hoping it'll remain an unsolved mystery."

As if to discourage such hopes, there came the dulcet sound of small-arms fire, repeated thrice. As Longarm's distress signal echoed back and forth from bank to bank, the pilot swore again and added, "Sounded like a pistol. Three shots in a row from anything means a cry for help, and you'd best throw another log on the fire, Curly."

The engineer left, muttering to himself, as Pop Fagan asked if there was anything he could do to help. Crawdad grunted, "You might see if you could pick up anything out ahead with the searching lamp. You know how to light her, don't you?"

The old theatrical trouper assured the river pilot he knew all about bright lights as, moving over to the big brass searching lamp to the right of the wheel, he struck a match to prove it.

The searching lantern was about the size and power of a locomotive headlamp, mounted on gimbals and provided with hand grips to swing it all about despite its mass. Fagan opened the side, lit the oil wick, adjusted the mantle of thorium mesh to glow white hot between the concave mirror and bull's-eye lens, and decided, as the beam lanced out through the wheelhouse glass to illuminate a big flat circle of muddy surface, "There's nothing there."

"Sweep to port, that's to your left," the pilot suggested in a disgusted voice. So Fagan did, and as Crawfish had already noticed, if not in as much detail, a human figure was heading their way on one hand and both knees aboard a bobbing raft of some sort.

The crusty pilot signaled for dead-in-the-current and deck-watch-forward as he made rude remarks about the maternal ancestry of a man he could barely see, thanks to the way Pop Fagan kept losing the raft with his wavering beam. But Longarm could see the showboat well enough as illuminated doors and windows opened the whole length of her cabin deck and, better yet, a heavyset cuss on the lower deck threw an uncoiling wheel of rope with more skill than courtesy as he hoarsely shouted, "Grab holt of this, you poor shipwrecked bastard."

So Longarm did, and the current naturally swung him and his flat mass of soggy timber against the hull of the showboat with a pretty good thud. But two other deckhands, figuring where he'd hit, were there to grab hold and haul him aboard as the remains of the other steamer's wheelhouse bobbed on past the side paddles and out of Longarm's life forever after likely saving it.

As the deckhands stood him straighter in his still-soggy boots, the chief engineer, Curly, joined them to demand an explanation.

Longarm told them, truthfully, he'd been aboard the *Prairie Rose,* that she'd blown one or both boilers, and that as far as he knew he was the only survivor.

Curly said, "Mebbe. You'd best hand over that gun you was just firing. Then I'd best take you topside to see what the pilot and owner want us to do with you."

Longarm started to argue, reflected on the derringer he still had as an ace in the hole, and politely removed the Webley from its sneaky shoulder holster to hand over by its stubby barrel. As he did so the burly engineer grunted, "You're dressed like a riverboat man too. Sometimes gents like you get blowed off steamboats, and sometimes the skipper puts 'em off on a sandbar or raft to teach 'em a lesson, if you follows my drift."

Longarm nodded soberly and replied, "If I hadn't been following your drift I'd have given you more of an argument. I know about card cheats and such left stranded by the management. Ain't it the usual custom to disarm such riffraff first?"

Curly smiled thinly and said, "I just did. Let's go topside, Mister—ah . . . ?"

"Some of my friends call me Brazo," Longarm decided, for now. The surly boss of the black gang was likely just behaving natural for his breed. On the other hand, like that derringer, a federal badge made a better ace in the hole when you kept just what you might be packing to your own fool self.

Meanwhile, this big old showboat was one hell of an improvement on that half-submerged roofing he'd been bobbing about on since the explosion. As he allowed the engineer to frog-march him up some stairs, he felt the improvement picking up speed, which made things even better, even if they weren't moving half as fast as the poor old *Prairie Rose* had been at the last.

He told Curly as much as they passed a knot of oddly dressed folk gathered on the cabin deck. Curly indicated a ladder and grunted, "Tell 'em about it topside. I know Turk Mason of old. He's loco enough to race after dark with the river falling. But so far, he's never had a boiler explosion afore."

Longarm dryly asked how often the same pilot was apt to enjoy such an experience. Curly chuckled despite himself and replied, "Only one to a customer. But like I said, there's more'n one way to wind up on a raft in these waters."

They climbed atop the wide flat Texas and strode toward the wheelhouse, perched like a toolshed atop the Texas with the tall black funnels rising to either side just ahead. As they approached, a short white-headed man wearing a dark suit and peaked cap popped out the back as if he thought he was a cuckoo clock figurine, calling out, "Welcome aboard *Captain Fagan's Floating Follies*. Captain Horatio Fagan at your service, unless you'd rather call me Pop. Crawdad wants to know if you're it or if we have to sweep for other castaways."

Longarm guessed right off that anyone called Crawdad had to be a river pilot. Any fool could run aground on the Big Muddy. It took the reflexes of a Crawdad, or crayfish, to back off a sandbank at first scrape, before the current could set your boxy hull more solidly. So as he followed the older gent inside he announced loud enough for the dark figure at the wheel to hear, "I've been adrift for the better part of an hour, atop the top of her wheelhouse. I have

87

called and I have called, and nobody answered. So add it up and do whatever you feel you ought to."

Crawdad Cartier growled, "I feel we ought to just keep going if we ever mean to make Sioux City this night. You others can be on record that this gent assured us he was the sole survivor."

"If he ain't been lying through his teeth," Curly amended. "Neither Turk nor Captain Gilchrist have ever blowed themselves up afore. But they've been knowed to leave a double-dealer stranded on a sandbar now and again."

Longarm thought about reminding them he'd been hauled off the roof of a wheelhouse rather than a sandbar. He even considered showing them his badge. Then he had a better idea and said, "Seeing we're so interested in riverboat wagers, would anyone here like to bet me a hundred that this boat won't reach the Sioux City landing ahead of the *Prairie Rose*?"

Pop Fagan said, "That's just silly, son. That quick-stepping sternwheeler passes us hours ago and . . . Oh, I see what you mean."

At the wheel beyond him, Crawdad grudgingly agreed. "Like the song says, 'Farther along we'll know more about it.' If they ain't made it to Sioux City by the time we get there, we'll know they went down somewheres betwixt Sioux City and the last time we sighted 'em way the hell south of here."

Longarm asked if he could use the searching lamp, saying, "I don't see how that wheelhouse roof I was on could have been the only trace of the *Prairie Rose* that floated."

Crawdad said, "Shine her straight ahead and hold her there. I likes to see where I'm going when someone tells me there's a boat on the bottom. Curly, I want me a hand up forward with a lead line too."

Curly protested, "We're in the main channel below Dakota Bend."

But the pilot insisted, "I know where the bottom of this channel is supposed to be. I want to know where the top of a sunken steamer might be afore I finds out the hard way, damn it!"

Curly said, "I'll post a linesman. What about this cuss?"

Crawdad answered, "What about him? You took his gun off him, didn't you? He may as well stay here with us for now. We'll want him handy, one way or the other, when we put in to Sioux City."

Curly nodded grimly and told Longarm, "Stay here, then, and do just as you're told. You know the trouble you're in if we find the *Prairie Rose* beat us that far up the river safe and sound, don't you?"

Before Longarm had to come up with an answer, the pilot swore and said, "*Somebody* sure as shit never made her to Sioux City tonight! Swing that beam to starboard, where the moon's shining down on that big silky slick, ah, Brazo."

Longarm did as he was told. The lamplight didn't reveal any floating wreckage. Anything that had surfaced had long since been swept south by the current. But machine oil, a heap of machine oil, still rose in rainbow blobs where the water boiled up and over something not too far below the surface.

Crawdad swore and said, "Aw, shit, now we're going to have to mark her with an anchored spar buoy, at least, and how'll we ever make Sioux City this side of moonset now?"

Pop Fagan replied, "At least this young feller was telling us true. Don't you feel better, knowing another boat just went down with all hands?"

Chapter 12

It was close, but they finally made Sioux City without having to tie up along the bank when they lost the full moon. For by that time they were above the last treacherous stretch below the well-situated landing and the eastern sky above the Iowa shore was light enough for Crawdad to steer by.

As the showboat slid her flat belly up on the landing, the shore crew assured them the *Morning Star,* with Captain Grimes, had indeed come and gone while nobody had seen hide nor hair of the *Prairie Rose.* So they gave Longarm's gun back and he strode ashore to scout up a Western Union facility in the wee small hours of a cold gray dawn.

It wasn't tough to find one. For unlike Council Bluffs across the river from Omaha, Sioux City took itself seriously.

The seat of Woodbury County, Iowa, was a busy meatpacking and transshipping point where the Missouri, Big Sioux, and Floyd rivers met up with half a dozen railroads great and small. The telegraph office was near the monument to Charles Floyd, who'd scouted the crossing for Lewis and Clark way back when. They'd named lots of other stuff after War Eagle, a local chief of the nation they'd sort of slandered by calling Sioux, or enemies. War Eagle, despite his handle, had been a fairly peaceable gent, still remembered fondly by old-timers.

The red-eyed clerk behind the counter in the all-night telegraph office took charge of the yellow telegram form Longarm filled out for his home office. He had to read it to determine how much it was apt to cost anyone. He read Longarm's handle twice, nodded, and confided, "I have a message for you as well, Deputy Long. Sent care of our Omaha office or, failing that'n, this'n. Would you like to read it?"

Longarm said reading wires from Denver had to have just guessing at their contents beat. So the clerk rummaged under the counter a spell, suppressing a yawn, and at last produced the wire Billy Vail had surely sent about this time the day before. As Longarm scanned it the clerk said, "You likely won't want me to send what you just wrote, seeing it can't be right, right?"

Longarm growled, "You just send what I just asked you to send and let us worry about who's right or wrong, damn it."

The clerk shrugged and replied, "If you say so. But I fail to see how you could have just drowned that Lucky Lovelace you were sent after if your boss thinks he left Cairo aboard another boat called the *Morning Star*. Didn't you say you and your man fell off the *Prairie Rose* together?"

"Send the damned wire the way I wrote it," Longarm insisted. He added, "Day rates, collect," as he turned away to stomp out, scowling fit to bust.

On the walk outside he encountered a more cheerful-looking individual who flashed a gilt star at him, saying, "Morning. I'd be Jeff Blue for Woodbury County, and they told me to look for a tall drink of water wearing no hat and a mighty wrinkled outfit."

Longarm identified himself and asked if they could carry on from there over breakfast. Deputy Blue said the Greek down the way served both his eggs and coffee mighty strong, and as they headed that way Longarm observed he'd yet to be poisoned or for that matter served a memorable meal in a greasy spoon of the Hellenic persuasion. Blue said that was how come he'd suggested the place.

As the two of them strode in, they were served a suspicious look by a halfway-pretty fat gal behind the counter. As he caught a glimpse of himself in the reflective glass door of the pie safe behind her, Longarm followed her drift. Aside from being hatless and in need of a shave, he looked as if he'd slept the night in his once-dapper suit, in some not-too-tidy gutter. Deputy Blue was dressed more cow, with a Patterson Colt conversion slung serious down his right thigh. The waitress cheered considerably when Longarm snapped a silver dollar on her slate countertop and allowed he'd like two eggs fried on both sides over chili con carne. He said he'd like his wake-up java while he waited, and Deputy Blue said he'd have just a cup of the same.

The fat gal called their orders out in what had to be her own lingo, since it was Greek to Longarm. He wondered what else she'd said about them when a goat-faced individual with curly gray hair peered out from the kitchen at them through a bitty window. Since his conscience was clean and he'd given his damned order, Longarm proceeded to fill Blue in on his reasons for being in these parts and his adventures so far. Blue proved he'd been listening by asking, "What about that bounty-hunting gal and the jasper she left Omaha with?"

Longarm shrugged and said, "The wire as just caught up with me was sent from Denver before they could have got my own. I'll find out if my pals intercepted Miss Aura Lee and Paul Henderson when I get a reply to the message I just sent. The tip Billy Vail got about Lucky Lovelace leaving Cairo aboard the *Morning Star* may or may not have been worth warm spit. Either way, he must have transferred his slippery ass to the *Prairie Rose* somewhere betwixt Cairo and Council Bluffs. That'd be easy enough, as soon as you study on it."

The waitress brought their coffee as Blue frowned thoughtfully. "That could have been Lovelace you went swimming with just as the *Prairie Rose* was fixing to blow up. But what if it was someone else, and what about your orders to scout for Lovelace some more aboard the *Morning Star*?"

Longarm sipped some coffee. It was pretty good, brewed strong enough to satisfy a Turk, even though he'd never met a Greek who'd admit to admiring anything Turkish. The waitress seemed surprised to see he drank his coffee black. As Blue creamed and sugared his own cup Longarm said, "My boss expects me to carry out sensible orders, not blind obedience to honest mistakes. When he told me Lovelace was likely on another boat, he had no way of knowing the sneak had already spotted me on yet another. I've had more time than you to consider all the other sneaks who might have wanted me over the side last night, and nobody works half as good as Lovelace himself."

The waitress brought his eggs over chili con carne on a cheap attempt at blue-willow chinaware. The eggs did smell a mite sulfuric when one sniffed at them. But they tasted all right, and Longarm knew whatever it was that spoiled eggs was killed by serious frying. None of those bitty bugs that French chemist had discovered could live in chili con carne either. Longarm's somewhat peculiar tastes in grub were inspired as much by his tumbleweed existence and uncertain sanitation as they were by the taste buds he'd been born with. Nobody but a greenhorn who felt lucky ever ordered chicken salad or cream of mushroom soup off a cook he didn't know well enough to kiss.

Washing down some peppery grub with bitter brew, Longarm told the deputy to his left, "Nobody but the late Captain Gilchrist and his crew knew I was a lawman. I hadn't had a chance to get in bad as a fellow passenger with anyone else aboard, save for Lovelace in the flesh, if only I could figure out which one was him and how he figured out who or what I really was. I only talked to a few of the passengers, or crew for that matter. I didn't bet any money, deal one card, or wink at one gal. Nobody but a rascal with something to hide from the law, who knew I was the law, had any reason for coming at me that way."

As Longarm chewed some more, Blue observed, "You said Lovelace got that other lawman down Cairo way with a back-shot. What do you reckon inspired him to change his methods aboard that sternwheeler last night?"

Longarm swallowed. "I've had time to study on that as well. Most everyone aboard was out on deck. The stern paddles were making a heap of noise, but not enough noise to muffle a pistol shot. He'd have likely gotten away with just pushing me over the rail if I hadn't sort of shifted my weight just as he was making his move. He almost got away with it, even so. He did push me over the side, and I only managed to haul him after because he was a tad smaller than me, just as Lovelace has been described to us."

Blue sipped, sighed, and said, "Since he never come back up after the two of you wound up in the river, we'd best have everyone down the river look each and every body over as it surfaces and . . . Oh, shit."

Longarm nodded soberly and said, "*All* the bodies ought to pop back up, downstream, once they, ah, mellow some."

Blue frowned. "In that case, who's to say which particular swollen corpse wound up in the river however?"

To which Longarm could only reply, "I just said that. Sorting out the soggy stiffs promises to be mighty tedious in proportion to any final resolution. Kith and kin coming forward to claim some of the dear departed may eliminate at least some of the men, and naturally none of the female stiffs could be Lovelace. But just the same, I'm glad I won't have to look every damn one over as they fetch up on shore or sandbank betwixt here and New Orleans over the next few weeks!"

Blue grimaced, drained the last of his cup, and said that made two of them as he rose, adding he'd best get that last suggestion about cadavers claimed or unclaimed on the wire across the way.

He left a dime on the counter to pay for his coffee and please the plump waitress. Longarm wished him luck, and had gotten back to his breakfast by the time the man calling himself Deputy Blue had made it to the doorway. So he figured that was about as good a time as any to get it over and done with.

Even as his horny palm slapped the ivory grips of his big .45, the deadly deputy he was out to back-shoot had rolled his broad back to the startled waitress and dropped to one knee on the sawdust-covered tile floor. But Longarm's own snub-nosed sixgun was out and blazing, three times, to bounce the treacherous "Deputy Blue" against the doorjamb and from there to the floor, more numb with surprise and shock than hurting yet.

As the waitress screamed and the cook came out of his kitchen with a frying pan held high, Longarm snapped, "Simmer down, I'm the law and it's over!" He rose to reach his victim in two long strides to kick the Patterson into a far corner. Then he hunkered down beside the severely wounded sneak to add, conversationally, "I figure you're done for. If it's any comfort, you ought to black out afore the shock wears off. Since you can't hardly be with the local sheriff's department, is there anyone else you'd like us to get in touch with?"

The man he'd nailed through the liver, stomach, and one lung coughed weakly and managed, "Never mind who I really was. How'd you figure me out?"

Longarm reached for a smoke with his free hands as he explained, "I was watching you in the glass front of that pie safe. I wasn't sure before you started to draw, of course, but I did find it a tad suspicious that they let a big-city lawman dress so casual, since they make me wear an infernal frock coat and tie on duty back in Denver."

The downed gunslick smiled wistfully and muttered, "They warned me you were slick as snail sweat. I should have just throwed down on you on sight but, no, I had to see what I could larn off you first."

Longarm stuck the cheroot in his own teeth and thumb-nailed a matchhead alight. "You talked convincing enough, up to the last. The county, the state, and Army Engineers would have already wired news of the disaster up and down the river long before any deputy looked me up to pick nits. But seeing someone else wanted to know how I was doing with my own beeswax, what say you tell me who you really are and who you were really working for."

The so-called Deputy Blue murmured, "Not hardly. Even if I owed you more than a gut-shooting, it wouldn't be ethical. A man has his professional pride to consider."

Longarm said, "At the rate you're going you won't even rate a nom de guerre on your grave marker. You're fixing to wind up in a pauper's lime pit in Potter's Field, old son. If you can't tell us who sent you after me, can't you at least tell us where to send the body?"

The dying owlhoot rider smiled in a surprisingly boyish way and said, "You really are good, ain't you? But it ain't gonna work. We both know how easy it is to nail a man's knowed associates, once we know who the fuck he might be!"

Longarm warned, "Watch your mouth, ladies present." But then he saw the Greek waitress had lit out someplace and that the cuss on the floor was staring up at him sort of odd. Longarm waved the blunt muzzle of the Webley in front of the dead man's eyes to make sure he was dead as he looked. Then he got back to his feet, cheroot gripped in his teeth, and had the British sixgun reloaded and back in its shoulder rig by the time the Greek gal got back with a couple of more authentic-looking copper-badges.

Longarm had naturally pinned his own federal badge to the wilted lapel of his ruined suit by this time. So neither of the Sioux City roundsmen acted silly. One, in fact, said, "Say, that old boy on the floor describes a mite like a want we got posted over to headquarters."

He hunkered down, opened the front of the dead man's shirt, and laughed like a mean little kid before he explained, "It's him, a lawman turnt bad called Reb Hansen. This full-rigged clipper ship you just stopped with a shot across its bows proves it. Hansen served in the Confederate Navy during the war and it sort of went to his chest. He's wanted in Missouri, Kansas, and Nebraska for shooting folk for hire."

Longarm said that didn't surprise him much, and asked if anyone knew who the late Reb Hansen had been working for. The copper-badge who seemed to know got back up, saying, "He was discreet as well as deadly. Some say he worked for anyone willing to pay half up front and the rest when through, like that whore in that song about the ring-dang-doo. There's a pretty good bounty on the rascal, though."

The other copper-badge said, "Hey, I recall that wanted

flier now. Didn't the rich kin of a Kansas victim post a thousand on his murderous dead hide, or five hundred on his being took alive?"

The other copper-badge said that was about the size of it. So Longarm said, "I wish my boss approved of me putting in for such privately posted bounty money. But he even frowns on us putting in for federal rewards. So it's a good thing you boys were the ones who finally brung him to justice, right?"

The younger of the two local lawmen frowned and asked what on earth Longarm was talking about. But his older and wiser sidekick poked him in the ribs to hush him as he nodded soberly at Longarm and said, "I follow your drift, Uncle Sam. Why don't you just go on about your own no-doubt-more-important business? Marty and me can tidy up here."

Longarm unpinned his own badge and placed it back where it usually rode with his bill-fold and identification as he softly pointed out, "You're going to have to cut the cook and waitress here in for a share."

The Sioux City expert on such matters sighed and replied, "Don't try to teach your granny how to suck eggs. We'll take care of the precinct captain too, if you'd like to get going before we have to take care of half the town!"

Longarm said, "Well, I have to get a shave, and a new hat wouldn't kill me for that matter." So they shook on it and parted friendly. Longarm was mighty relieved to get out of all the paperwork it took to clear a simple shootout these days. He had to study some on what he was supposed to do about the sneak or sneaks the late Reb Hansen had been working for, though. Nobody he could come up with at short notice made a lick of sense.

Chapter 13

Seeing he had a perfectly good or leastways still servicable outfit just down the Big Muddy in Omaha, Longarm put himself back together more practical than pretty. He bought a plain cotton shirt and shoestring tie, along with a summer-weight planter's hat of glazed straw that would likely look all right till it got rained on a time or two. Then he found a tailor willing to spot-clean and press the dumb suit while he waited.

He liked himself a heap better as he viewed the results in a pier glass. He felt free to look and act more sensible, now that Billy Vail's grand notion of sneaking up on Lucky Lovelace had fallen through.

It reminded Longarm of that story about another doomed vessel, where the only one left is the whaler telling the tale after a great white whale gets done killing everyone else in the whole book.

Lighting another smoke out front as he tried to decide whether to go left or right, Longarm reconsidered that tip about Lovelace really being aboard the *Morning Star* all this time. Whether that was so or not, nobody had to dress half so fancy to ride with Captain Gloria Grimes. The problem would be catching up with old Gloria and her less fancy sternwheeler. For plain or fancy, she and old Jim Truman had to be way the hell up the Big Muddy by this time.

Longarm knew he could easily beat any steamboat up to Milk River by rail and just lay in wait there for Gloria and any uglier folk she might have on board. By this time word of the boiler explosion aboard the rival *Prairie Rose* had likely caught up with Gloria and she'd be setting a more sensible pace, knowing she had nobody out to humble her on a river getting shallower by the mile.

As he shook out his match Longarm grumbled, half aloud, "I could waste me many a day in Milk River only to discover Lovelace had never been aboard, or worse yet, that he'd been aboard but gotten off at any of a score or more landings along the way! Where in the Bill of Rights does it say a fleeing killer has to ride a steamboat all the way to the end of the line? If the son of a bitch left Cairo aboard either boat it was to get out of Cairo, not to get to Great Falls or anywhere else in particular!"

Longarm still headed for the railroad depot, though he felt undecided. It sounded tedious already, but if he took a local and got off at each stop past let's say . . . Shit, did the main line stop all along the upper Missouri, or was he thinking about spurs and crossings, in which case even his tedious notion wouldn't work!

He didn't know. They'd know at the depot. But two full city blocks this side of it he met up with Captain Fagan of the showboat. The old showman agreed Longarm's new hat was a peach and asked, "Have you by any chance seen our juvenile lead, Mister Sterling De Vere? He doesn't seem to be at any of the finer hotels here in town."

Longarm confessed he'd never seen anyone called Sterling De Vere in his life, as far as he knew, and asked why the cuss would have checked into any sort of Sioux City hotel if he had quarters aboard *Miss Baton Rouge*.

Captain Fagan said, "You must have seen him and all the others last night. They were all up forward when you and Curly came up to the wheelhouse. As to why he'd be staying here in Sioux City, I mean to ask him the moment I catch up with him. Anyone who quits a show in mid-tour is no trouper, even when he gives notice. Walking off without a word to anyone is downright spooky!"

Longarm agreed, but asked if by any chance their leading man had a drinking problem, or any other sort of problem that might have inspired him to light out for parts unknown.

Fagan grimaced and said, "I wouldn't be so worried about Sterling if he was a drunk or a troublemaker. I don't hire showfolk of that ilk. The lad came aboard at Saint Louis, highly recommended by a Chicago agent of repute. Since then he's gotten on well with the rest of the troupe, never missed his mark or flubbed a line, and—"

"Hold on," Longarm said, cutting in. "You say your missing actor is a new face on board, and that he came on board this side of Cairo?"

Fagan explained, "We have a certain amount of such turnover every tour. I swear I sometimes think some so-called actors are only interested in passage up and down the damned river. You don't suppose Sterling De Vere pulled that on us, do you?"

Longarm smiled thinly and opined, "A man who'd call himself Sterling De Vere would likely do most anything. But before I say anything as dumb, describe your missing silverware to me in more detail."

Fagan pursed his lips thoughtfully. "Well, to begin with he was about your height, mayhap a tad slimmer. I suppose most women would find you about as good-looking, in your own rough-hewn way. No juvenile lead would ever appear on stage with a mustache like your own, of course. And so, in sum, picture a tall handsome type, smooth shaven and, yes, quite a bit less broad across the chest and shoulders, once you consider he wears padded shoulders and you don't seem to."

Longarm pictured the missing actor fuzzy, to keep from fooling himself with false details, and then he shook his head and said, "Neither a Deputy Blue nor another cuss I'd be interested in fits that description worth mention. There's a Paul Henderson described as a tall handsome heartbreaker. But he left Omaha bound for El Paso via Denver at a time your Sterling character had to have been aboard your floating follies if he only got off here this morning. Are you sure about that, by the way? I mean, if he got off further down the river, without anyone noticing till just now . . . "

"He left the showboat here in Sioux City, shortly after you did this morning, as a matter of fact. The same deckhand saw you both stride down the same gangway. But tell me more about this Henderson person."

Longarm shook his head again. "Be a waste of your time and mine, Captain. We've already got enough of a mystery many a mile and going on twenty-four hours this side of a bounty huntress on the trail of that other rascal catching up with him in Omaha. So let's chaw some more on the tall cuss you're hunting. You say he was vouched for by some theatrical agent up Chicago way? How do you work that, by telegraph wires?"

Captain Fagan shook his worried gray head and confided, "Letters of reference. Everyone in my profession packs a scrapbook and all the letters of reference possible. We did have to shift some roles about when we decided to stage a revival of *Uncle Tom's Cabin*, thanks to all the Northeast farm folk who've come out this way to homestead of late. When we recast Dudley Drew as the villain instead of the hero and gave the part of Uncle Tom to our old villain, in blackface, of course—"

"Never mind all that. I've seen the play, more'n once," Longarm noted. "Is it safe to assume your one missing trouper, who won't fit as another riverboat traveler I had in mind, is the only fairly new face on board?"

Captain Fagan said, "Miss Blossom Bascom, who plays the piano and calliope with equal skill, came aboard just down the river as well, now that you mention it. But surely you don't suspect *her* of anything sinister?"

Longarm dryly observed the calliope playing he'd heard, so far, could hardly constitute anything more sinister than skipping a few music lessons in her girlhood.

The old showman winced and replied, "What can I say? We used to have a pretty good organist. He quit to play piano in a Memphis house of ill repute, and you have to admit Miss Blossom plays good enough to attract attention."

101

Longarm agreed their calliope was loud enough, at any rate, and said, "Speaking of riverboat ladies, I'm way more interested in Captain Gloria Grimes of the *Morning Star*. Last I heard, she was way out ahead of all of us, last night, before I wound up with you all."

Captain Fagan looked about, distracted, as he replied, "You told us all about that explosion aboard the *Prairie Rose*, and others have been pestering my crew about it all morning, as if we knew anything about it. Meanwhile, I have to stage *Uncle Tom's Cabin* this evening with or without that infernal Sterling De Vere. So tell me something, ah, Brazo, have you ever considered an acting career?"

Longarm laughed incredulously and replied, "As a matter of fact I once toured with a company, and there was an opera singer I was mighty fond of one time, and vice versa. But getting out there and making a fool of myself just ain't my style. Even if it was, do I look like Uncle Tom to you?"

Captain Fagan didn't smile back. He said, "I just told you we have that part cast. If we were to switch Dudley Drew back to the kindly father of Little Eva and cast you, with that villainous mustache, as Simon Legree . . ."

"I'd as soon try tightrope-walking across Niagara Falls!" Longarm declared. "I understand there's money in behaving *really* foolish, and I wouldn't feel half as dumb in pink tights on a tight wire!"

Before he could explain what he really did for a living, the older man insisted, "Simon Legree only appears in the last act and it's an easy part. You're a head taller than our Uncle Tom, so all you'll really have to do is loom over him with a big black whip whilst he cowers and begs for mercy. Uncle Tom has all the important lines."

Longarm frowned thoughtfully and replied, "Not in the book, as I recall from the last time I read it. In any case, I'm way more interested in catching up with Captain Gloria Grimes and anyone she may have aboard her *Morning Star*. I was on my way to buy me a railroad ticket up to Milk River, as a matter of fact."

Captain Fagan took him by one sleeve, insisting, "Wait. We'll be putting in at Milk River ourselves, and I know

Miss Gloria and her crew of old. Stick with us, give us a hand with our labor shortage until we can book a more devoted villain, and—"

"No offense," Longarm told him. "But you ain't about to catch up with the *Morning Star* in that big sidewheeler whether you stop along the way to give shows or not. That other boat has a day's lead on you already, and it only stops long enough to put passengers and freight off and on!"

Fagan nodded but said, "Miss Gloria's fighting to hold on to her mail contract and headwaters trade. She and her pilot will claw like wildcats trying to defend their record for miles gained despite the current we'll all be bucking on the upstream side of the Dakota line."

Longarm started to speak. The old-timer interrupted. "Hear me out. You say you want to catch up with that young sass and her sternwheeler, and I say you'd hardly be able to avoid it, sticking with me and mine. For while there's no doubt Miss Gloria will make it to the head of navigation by the time we get much further upstream than Yankton, what goes up must come down. Steaming *down* the upper Missouri presents a pilot with a whole new problem. He's inclined to set speed records with his paddles trying to back-water if he doesn't watch the boils and slicks ahead of him sharp."

"I know you go downstream almost as fast as a railroad train might manage," said Longarm, with a bemused frown.

Fagan smiled like a kid swiping apples and told him, "Jim Truman doesn't like to steam that sudden, save in broad daylight. On their return trips they tie up every night and make up for the lost time with the help of the current, once they can see where it's trying to carry 'em. As a rule Miss Gloria and her whole crew spend an evening aboard *Fagan's Floating Follies* whenever they encounter us on their downriver run. So why don't we just get on back to the landing and get you started on the few lines you'll have to memorize by this evening?"

Longarm was about to say no when he yelled, "Down!" instead, and when that didn't work, shoved the older man on his face in the mud behind a watering trough, whipping out

103

his own gun as, sure enough, a rifle ball ricocheted wetly off the scummy surface of the stock-water.

Then Longarm was down behind the same trough on one knee, punching holes in the false front above a hardware store across the way. He couldn't say whether he'd hit anyone either. Nobody on either side was shooting as police whistles chirped among the rapidly gathering crowd. Longarm had reloaded and put his own gun away before moving to help Captain Fagan back up. He'd just finished doing that when a burly copper-badge bulled through the crowd to demand some explanation for all that noise on a work day in the middle of such a grand city.

Longarm pointed at the rooftops across the way and replied, "It wasn't our fault. Me and the captain, here, were just jawing peaceable when some jasper wearing a derby hat and rifle rose behind that hardware store's false front to peg a shot at us. Lucky for us, I spotted the flash of sunlight on his barrel in time, and even luckier, he must have been aiming a single-shot Hawkins or Sharps our way. Slug sounded like a .50 or even a .52 buffalo round."

The copper-badge stared thoughtfully across the way. "He must have only wanted one of you bad, then."

Longarm nodded soberly. "That's what I just said."

A helpful onlooker volunteered, "I heard the shot and seen the sniper running off across the roof like Santa Claus, Constable. Like this young feller says, he had on a derby. I can't say what breed of buffalo gun that was in his hands, though, save for the fact it was a long-barreled widow-maker indeed."

Longarm was braced for the local lawman to get around to the subject of his own hardware. Most towns the size of this one had pesky pistol ordinances these days. But before he had to produce his own identification and gun permit, the copper-badge was asking Fagan who the both of them might be. So Longarm kept still and let the captain identify them both as members of the showboat troupe, and even better, the copper-badge recalled the *Floating Follies* from the last time it had put on a show in these parts.

He said, "I've heard of throwing rotten eggs and spoilt tomaters at actors. But buffalo rounds are surely overdoing it. Do you have any notion who might have it in for you that bad, Captain?"

Fagan shook his head with the expression of a kid being sent to bed early for no damned reason at all as he replied, "We haven't even caught a fresh egg in recent memory. What about some sort of religious fanatic? You know how some hellfire-and-damnation preachers carry on about our life upon the wicked stage, as they imagine it."

The copper-badge shrugged and said, "We got all sorts of odd folk with odd notions in Iowa these days. I don't see how we'll ever know for sure, unless he tries again. Meanwhile, I'd find me some cover and lay low a spell if I had a lunatic stalking *me* with a buffalo gun!"

Captain Fagan gulped and said, "You surely paint a pretty picture, Constable. But let's hope it was just a lunatic choosing his targets at random from among the madding crowd. For the show must go on, and I don't see how we'd ever be able to search every ticket holder for concealed weapons."

Neither Longarm nor the local lawman asked how come the show had to go on. Fagan had just said they sold tickets, and when you failed to put on a show you had to give the money back.

The older man told Longarm, "I'm going back to the landing and to hell with our missing actor." Then Fagan blinked and added, "Say, you don't suppose that could have been Sterling shooting at us just now, do you?"

Longarm couldn't say. He had no idea what the missing De Vere looked like, or how come he was missing. He did know a known gunslick had already tried to kill him that very morning. So it seemed obvious that one ball from a single-shot rifle had never been meant for old Fagan.

In any event, when Fagan repeated his suggestion that Longarm tag along with his showboat troupe in hopes of meeting most anyone up to anything along the Big Muddy, Longarm decided, "Why not? Like you just said, potshots are mighty confusing amongst a madding crowd, and I've some time to kill before I can head back to Denver whether anyone starts up with me again or not."

Fagan was only half listening. He said, "Let's go. We have to get you to beating Uncle Tom convincingly before the curtain goes up this very evening!"

Chapter 14

They couldn't, of course. Longarm tried his awkward best but he wasn't even able to get all the others in the cast of the play straight in his head in the time they had to work with. Being up on a stage was a heap more confusing than it looked from the audience. A lot of stuff went on off to one side, with actors and stage help trying not to cuss one another as they tore around behind the scenery, shifted the scenery, and even changed their duds and makeup in front of God and everybody.

There were many more folk in the tale of Uncle Tom than Captain Fagan could afford to pay, even if one showboat had held quarters on its cabin deck for *that* madding a crowd. So some of the better, or at least more experienced, actors had to play more than one part, and it sure was scandalous, watching women shuck out of one dress and into another, just off to one side, till one got used to it and noticed nothing more important than bare limbs that showed enough to matter. It was likely the cussing that went with the changing that made the sideshow seem so bawdy. Once you got used to it, it was more comical than shocking to hear Miss Blanche Balmoral, changing from Little Eva to the heroic Eliza, snapping, "Not in my eye, you asshole!" when the makeup man changed her from a sweet little blonde to a colored gal, with a heap of what looked like chocolate custard and a frizzy black wig.

They would only do one dress rehearsal, likely to save wear and tear on everyone's nerves as well as their costumes. So Longarm got to run through his own short part in just his pants and shirtsleeves, albeit several times, with the middle-aged Allan Eldrich, who looked like an English butler when he pretended to be Uncle Tom, the noble darky, without any makeup.

But it wasn't another white man sobbing, "Don't beat me, Massah Legree!" that inspired Longarm to snicker where he was supposed to be sneering. They were putting on the play ass-backwards from the way Mrs. Harriet Beecher Stowe had written her pretty good book back before the war. Suddenly the noble darky cussed him, saying, "Goddamn it, Brazo, you're supposed to be a Southern slave driver. Why are you putting on that phoney New England accent? That's not the way you talk to begin with, you simp!"

Longarm nodded and said, "I know. I was born and reared in West-By-God-Virginia and I've been riding with other country boys since I come West after the war. But you see, in the book, Simon Legree was a Yankee from up North. Part of the trouble he had with Tom was that he just didn't know how to tell a gentleman of color from an uppity coon. So when a dignified lay preacher like Uncle Tom falls into his clutches—"

"Oh, my sweet shit!" moaned Little Eva or the thirty-odd-year-old Blanche Balmoral from the wings. "First we have to show him how to hit his mark, then he still enters stage right like a cowhand arriving at a barn dance, and now he wants to tell us the fucking motivation of the fucking heavy!"

As everyone but Longarm laughed, the brassy unnatural blonde strode out to him, demanded his prop whip, and snapped, "This is all you have to do, you asshole. Get in character, Allan."

Eldrich wiped the sardonic smile from his pale lips and cowered before the petite actress as if she stood nine feet tall, whimpering, "Don't beat me, Massah Legree!" Longarm had to shake his head, again, even though Blanche Balmoral sounded villainous as hell, snarling, "Then tell me what I wish to know, Tom! Where are those other slaves hiding! Tell me or I'll flay you alive with this big black whip!"

Longarm protested, "Hold on, ma'am. That ain't the way the story goes at all! Uncle Tom never carries on like no crybaby. The whole point of this here scene is that a noble slave has the chance to save himself if only he'll knuckle under and betray other slaves to Simon Legree. He gets that last fatal beating when he *defies* the brutal and not-too-bright slave driver."

"How would you like me to smack you with this whip for real?" asked the sweet-looking but bitch-eyed blonde in a lightweight summer smock. As she started to go on about smart-ass rubes who couldn't even master a walk-on part, the somewhat younger actress who played a mean white gal or the impish black Topsy, depending, joined them to murmur, "Let me see what I can do, Blanche. Come out on deck with me a moment, Brazo. We'd better talk."

He went with her willingly enough, even though someone behind suggested she shove him overboard, for her light brown hair was natural and she had the shape to play either a mature white lady in one of the early acts or a slave girl just starting to bud and likely doomed to a life of perdition after neither Little Eva nor Uncle Tom was there to keep her on the straight and narrow anymore.

Offstage she was known as Vania Du Val. Longarm was too polite to ask what her real name might be. He'd noticed show folk seemed to make up names no real human being would ever wind up with, but what the hell, he had 'em all calling him Brazo and, so far, nobody had been rude enough to ask how come.

As she walked him back toward the stern, facing the river, Vania explained, "Reading a book is one thing and watching a staged play is another. I'm sure that in adapting *Uncle Tom* from a longish magazine serial to an evening's entertainment they had to simplify things just a teeny-weeny bit."

Longarm nodded but said, "I know that. I ain't stupid. In his *Henry the Fifth*, Shakespeare comes right out and asks the audience to imagine a handful of actors on foot are two whole armies, mounted on noble steeds. I know you got to whittle whole chapters out of a book, and even get rid of half the characters to shoehorn even a shorter novel onto a bigger stage than the one you folks have to work with. But just the same, the basic notion of *Uncle Tom* can be told the way it was meant without all that weeping and wailing. I've seen stage productions of *Uncle Tom's Cabin* before. Next to the book they were all mighty dumb. A body knowing the story from just the play would think poor Mrs. Stowe was a silly sentimental female, when in point of fact she wrote a pretty sensible tale, at least as good as *Moby Dick*."

Vania glanced thoughtfully up at him to murmur, "I share your views about silly sentimental writing, and to tell the truth, I've always thought that was about the sum total of *Uncle Tom's Cabin*. The book, I fear, was before my time, and having played in the play, I never felt up to reading it."

He nodded, and as she leaned back against the rail he told her, "I doubt you could have been born when the book was first published back in '51. Putting it on as a play came way later, after the book had helped start the war, according to Abe Lincoln when he finally met up with the lady who wrote it."

She said, "I'd heard that. I've never quite understood it. Poor old Uncle Tom just gets into one sorry scrape after another until in the end most everyone in the cast is dead. The end."

Longarm shook his head and said, "That's what I was arguing about in there. Harriet Beecher Stowe spent some time in her girlhood on a Southern plantation, run by friends even *she* had to recognize as decent folk who treated their slaves no worse than if they'd been white hired help. Before things got so tense betwixt the states, a lot of folks, North and South, excused the peculiar institution by pointing to all the happy darkies living on properly run plantations."

"You'd never get that idea from *Uncle Tom's Cabin*," she sighed.

He said, "The play misses Miss Harriet's point. She set out to show it was the *system itself* that was capricious and

110

cruel. In the book, that villain they want me to play is only an inevitable result, no matter how hard decent white folk try to justify letting anyone have that much power over the lives of others."

She leaned back and asked him to go on. She sounded as if she meant it. So he said, "Uncle Tom and his children start out happy enough on a plantation owned by the enlightened Shelby family. The friendly masters allowed Tom to learn to read and his grown daughter, Eliza, has been allowed to marry up in church, same as any free white gal."

Vania nodded. "Eliza's played by Blanche after she gets to die as Little Eva."

Longarm nodded. "She and her baby escape to Canada near the end. Before that happens the kindly Shelbys fall on hard times and have to sell their slaves, splitting up Uncle Tom's family among different new owners, good, bad, or indifferent. Tom is sold to a dealer who's taking him down to New Orleans aboard a boat a lot like this one when little Eva Saint Clare, the only child of a wealthy planter, falls over the side."

Vania nodded and said, "We have that in the play. Uncle Tom saves Little Eva and Saint Clare purchases him in gratitude."

"The deal was that Saint Clare meant to set Uncle Tom free, and the hell of it is, he means it. Only one thing and another keep coming up, and meanwhile, old Tom's treated decent enough on the Saint Clare plantation. Little Eva, that's Miss Blanche, is an angelic child and her little colored pal, Topsy, that's you, both call him Uncle Tom."

"Then the angels come to take Little Eva away to heaven," said the white girl who'd play the younger Topsy that evening if Captain Fagan had anything to say about it.

Longarm nodded. "That's where the play skips way too much. Little Eva dies and Tom just sucks his thumb till Simon Legree starts beating on him for no sensible reason. In the book things take way longer to go to hell in a hack. Saint Clare is a decent man, the sort of master lots of real masters liked to think they were, and Tom is his true friend who shares his grief. So he doesn't pester Saint Clare about his freedom whilst the poor heart-busted cuss is nursing his grief with way more liquor than common sense. He's lost first his wife and now their only child. Tom figures signing those papers setting him free can wait."

"But then Saint Clare is killed too," said Vania, eyes bright with renewed understanding. "I see what you mean. Everyone means well, but it's so easy for things to go wrong."

Longarm said, "It was Harriet Beecher Stowe's meaning, Miss Vania. Saint Clare's unexpected death, owing money against the next cotton crop, results in Tom being sold yet again. Simon Legree is more a bewildered bully than a villain with a sensible motive. He sees Tom has the respect of the other slaves. He tries to enlist Tom as a sort of fellow villain. When Tom refuses to betray his own kind, Legree takes his spite out on him. Tom doesn't carry on hysterical. He dies about as dignified as a man can manage, being beaten to death. Then good old George Shelby, who would have been played by your Sterling De Vere tonight if he hadn't run off like Eliza, shows up just too late to save Tom and vows a vow to stomp out slavery, starting now."

Longarm looked away and softly added, "There was more to the war than that alone, of course, but it sure took more dying than Uncle Tom ever managed, alone, to change the way things had always been."

She softly murmured, "I know. My father and two uncles fell at Chickamauga, and I remember my mamma telling my dad she'd never speak to him again if he did anything that mean. One of my uncles left a wife and kids to mourn him too. But we were talking about another uncle, called Tom. If I say I see why you feel the stage version is all wrong, will you say you'll try to get your few lines right by this evening?"

He laughed and said, "May as well. I can see it's too late to rewrite the fool play, even if I knew how."

So she kissed him on the cheek and led him back inside by one hand. Nobody else said anything, and the next time he had to talk mean to Uncle Tom he was able to do so without breaking up. For his mind was more on the meaning of that peck on the cheek than dumb old Eldrich begging for mercy.

But whatever that doubtless sisterly kiss might have meant, he laughed like hell at dress rehearsal when Eldrich went through the same fool lines and motions painted black as the ace of spades.

Chapter 15

He'd recovered, or hoped he had, by the time the sun was setting on the far side of the river and they all had to get things right or give everyone their money back.

As Sioux City townsfolk filed aboard in the gloaming, the calliope was blaring a fair rendition of "Lorena" up forward. Nobody but the show folk were allowed up on the cabin deck, of course, and while Longarm was in his Simon Legree outfit, with that Webley bulldog under the deliberately dirty-looking jacket, just in case, he knew he wouldn't have to torture anyone until the last act, and so, "Lorena" being one of his favorite songs from long ago, he ambled up toward the steam-powered calliope to see if Miss Blossom Bascom really knew any other tunes. He'd suspected, or hoped, she might be another female musician called Red Robin the first time he'd heard her playing in the sticks. But as he'd already noticed earlier, Miss Blossom was a real blonde starting to spread just a mite where she sat down, but plumped just right above the waist. He didn't know whether they'd named her after the way she looked or whether she'd grown to womanhood inspired by the name. Either way, her little rosebud mouth seemed about to blossom into something far more lush any minute. Her big blue eyes held a heap of restrained surprises too, one suspected.

As he came around the brass pipes of her calliope, she glanced up at him, dovelike hand fluttering all over the organlike keyboard. Like many professional musicians, Blossom knew the trick of talking through rather than over the almost ear-splitting pitch of her pipes.

He still had to ask her to repeat it before he understood her to mean she felt the steam pressure was too low. You surely couldn't tell from where he was standing. Forcing himself to answer deep in his chest instead of screaming, he asked her if she wanted him to scout up the engineer and ask them to throw another few scoops in the firebox. She shook her blond curls and said, "I already asked. Curly says I've all the pressure I need, the mean thing."

Longarm didn't want to take sides about that. He knew Curly could be surly. At the same time he couldn't help noticing her playing sounded more in pitch this evening. He said soothingly, "It ain't as if anyone has to hear you clear across the river. We're right against the shore, and Curly could be worried about glass windows. Do you know the one about the mocking bird on Sweet Hattie's grave?"

She nodded. "Of course. It's among my campfire songs of the G.A.R., albeit I'm sure the rebel army sang it too. I get lots of requests for that one, this one, and 'Aura Lee' from older gents who rode on both sides. Were you ever a soldier, ah, Brazo?"

He muttered something about scouting Shoshone for the cavalry a short spell back. The damned old war he'd run off to while in his teens hadn't been over much more than fifteen years and already gals were referring to men who'd fought in it as older gents. He supposed, to a gal who'd have been, say, six or eight at the time, it *had* been quite a spell back. He had to smile as he considered the plight of old boys who'd really done wonders and eaten cucumbers in that or any other war. A hero coming home with one arm in a sling and ribbons all over his chest no doubt got to be the bee's knees with the gals back home for, oh, seven years tops. Then, if he was still single, and still bragging, pretty little things who'd been too young for him to fool with in his heroic days had him figured as a dirty old man if he fooled with 'em now, no matter how young he might still feel.

Gliding gracefully into the dirge about that mocking bird on Sweet Hattie's grave, Miss Blossom asked him if he knew the words. He did, but said he only recalled the soldiers camped down the road singing it when he was an impressionable youth.

She laughed and said, "Soldiers are more sentimental than cowboys when it comes to ballads about lost loves. They never seem to really care that they never got the girl of their dreams. Wouldn't you think they'd prefer happy songs as they march off to meet the foe?"

He didn't answer. He didn't want to go into girls the boys in blue or gray might have left behind with a lady who couldn't have been old enough to worry about that way at the time. So she never got to hear his simple explanation, assuming he had it right.

He was pretty sure he did, having sadly sung about Lorena, Aura Lee, and all those other lovely ghosts just before or after yet another bloodletting like Shiloh. The wistful feelings inspired by thoughts of lost lovers were survivable. They hurt enough to take one's mind off other hurts that might not be. It was Hattie's grave, not your own, that mocking bird was singing over. It was Lorena, not your right leg, you'd never see again. And what the hell, in the end he really *had* wound up in bed with at least one Aura Lee, whether she was still alive right now or not. He knew he'd get no chance to check with Western Union about that till after the show. He told Blossom Bascom to keep up the good work, and moved aft to the inside stairway leading down to the backstage area on the main deck.

On the way Curly, the engineer, almost bumped into him, on purpose, to growl, "Where have you been, with which one, this time? Miss Vania and Miss Blossom are both spoken for. So watch it!"

Longarm smiled easily and replied, "It's nice to know someone's watching me that close. Since you seem to feel you've been appointed the guardian of public morals aboard

116

this vessel, Curly, be advised Miss Vania wanted to talk to me about my part in the fool play and Miss Blossom needs more pressure for her steam organ."

Curly grimaced and said, "I've been bleeding steam to that same calliope since long afore she come aboard and I suspicion I know how much pressure it needs. We tried it her way, more'n once. Too much pressure throws the pipes off pitch."

Longarm said, "At the risk of making you cross your legs, I agree with you about that, Curly. Does this mean we're having a hot love affair?"

Curly blinked and blurted out, "Hold on! Are you trying to make me out some sort of queer-boy who likes other men in the Biblical sense?"

Longarm shook his head. "Just trying to show you how dumb it sounds to accuse everyone having an innocent conversation of dirty thoughts. We have nothing to argue about, Curly. So don't argue with me. I mean it. In case Captain Fagan failed to inform you, I've had more than one shot pegged at me since someone shoved me over the rail of a steamboat, and I don't mind telling you I feel proddy as a bear with a toothache at the moment."

"Are you saying I had something to do with them attempts upon your life, Brazo?" growled Curly.

Longarm growled back. "I'm not even thinking about you one lick more than I have to. So don't make me have to. I just told you someone a lot scarier than you has started up with me more than once. I mean to kill anyone who starts up with me again, and like the old Indian said, I have spoken. Now get out of my way or fill your fist."

Curly got out of the way, muttering something about not being armed for Gawd's sake. Longarm didn't see fit to warn him that made him even dumber. They said young Henry McCarthy a.k.a. Billy the Kid had blown away a colored blacksmith who'd come at the kid unarmed. A lot of good it had done the blacksmith, acting like such a total asshole in country where even the whores packed guns.

Down below, behind the drawn curtains, total chaos ruled, or seemed to, as folk dressed outlandishly dashed about in the semi-darkness. He spied Vania over by the stage curtains, dressed and made up as the older white lady she'd play in the first act. He joined her as he saw she was peeking through a slit in the curtains. When he asked her how come, she murmured, "Counting the house. It's a large audience tonight. How are you feeling about your debut as Simon Legree?"

He said, "Stupid. If I mayhap had more time to get set, I'd feel more sure of myself. But it seems I've barely been over all those lines one time and it's already time to say 'em in front of a whole herd of strangers."

She smiled wistfully and said, "You'll be raring to go by the time we get to the last act of the main performance. First we warm them up with some singing, dancing, and juggling. It'll feel like a million years, and you'll be anxious to get it over with by the time you go on."

He asked to peek. She let him. There was quite a crowd out front, as she'd said. It was hard to make out individual faces. When he said so, she nodded and explained, "The light's supposed to shine *our* way, not *their* way. They pay to see *us*, see?"

He frowned and muttered, "I'm only worried about one or two of 'em really out to boo me. Captain Fagan said there was no practical way to search everybody for weapons as they filed aboard. Does anybody keep an eye peeled for more obvious savagery?"

She dimpled and replied, "Define savagery. We play more than one Indian agency along this river. I'm not sure what the Sioux think Uncle Tom and Topsy are."

He shook his head and said, "They know. Most medicine men can read our newspapers. Makes 'em seem more in touch with the spirits when they predict particularly dumb Indian policy. Indians took sides in the war as well, with the Cherokee backing the South and the Osage lifting hair for the North whilst Red Cloud and Little Crow led the so-called Sioux against us in general. They call a colored gent a *wasichu sapa* or black white man in Lakota. Yet Indians have been known to spare slaves, back when some officers still had slaves out our way. So all in all, I'd say most

Indians grasp our ways way better than most of us grasp *their* ways."

Vania wrinkled her pert nose and said, "I confess you left me confused about my part as Topsy, explaining the concept of the plot so well to me before. As I play her, she's a comic figure. Is that the way Miss Harriet meant her part to be?"

Longarm shrugged and asked, "What's that fancy way of saying funny and pathetic at the same time?"

When she suggested, "Tragi-comic," he nodded and said, "Yep, that's old Topsy, then. In the book she's a pretty little black gal with neither manners nor morals worth mention. She's an orphan who just sort of growed, untutored and undisciplined, till Saint Clare makes her a sort of playmate for Little Eva. Uncle Tom helps. Topsy means well. She's just wild and immoral by birthright, see?"

Vania stared up at him big-eyed as the weed child she'd be playing later as she replied, "Oh, I do see! In the play, Topsy's just a silly played for comic relief. But in real life, I mean the real novel based on real life, she had the chance to grow up as a more refined young lady of color, only with Eva dead and Tom sold down the river . . . "

"That's about the size of it." He nodded as Captain Fagan, wearing his master of ceremonies outfit, herded them both into the wings with a warning about the curtain going up.

In point of fact two curtains parted. A showboat didn't have the elaborate stage machinery of even a modest playhouse on shore. Since the *Floating Follies* had begun as an all-purpose sidewheeler, the audience sat facing the stage on the cargo deck. The resulting overhead didn't leave enough room for a proper balcony, let alone the overhead fly space for curtains or back cloths moving up and down. There was a sort of half-assed attempt at raised seats at the rear of the audience. Folks perched back there looked sort of like a panel sitting in an unusually tall jury box. Stage scenery had to be folded out on the stage from either side. So Longarm got to lean against a flat fake forest as he watched McArtle and McAuley, dressed in green like they lived under a toadstool, sing and clog dance at the same time. He had to wonder what any Indians up the river a piece would make out of that.

Then Dudley Drew, if Longarm had his name straight, came on stage to throw Indian clubs all over the place without letting any get away completely. Up until then Longarm had thought Dudley Drew was going to play Little Eva's kindly father tonight. Then he reflected that still worked as long as old Dudley didn't hit himself in the head with any of those whirling clubs. Saint Clare showed up in the second act. So Drew would have plenty of time to get his wind back and change duds.

Figuring nobody in the cast was likely to be behind the repeated attempts against him, Longarm let his attention shift out front, where in point of fact he couldn't see one hell of a lot.

Closer in, just off to one side of the footlights, he saw that was pretty little Blossom Bascom tinkling the piano instead of her steam calliope as old Dudley Drew threw those clubs up out of sight and then caught 'em again as they whirled down from behind the pasteboard proscenium arch. She sounded more skilled on the piano. A steam organ in this confined space might have been overdoing it in any case.

His old pal, Red Robin, had spread a mite when she sat down after sitting at a piano all over the West. Blossom's somewhat broader butt no doubt accounted for her playing somewhat better. They said practice made perfect. He didn't want to think about the way both she and old Red Robin might be built by the time they got to hitting every note as writ. He didn't want to think about either gal's broad ass if he meant to go out on that fool stage without a hard-on later.

He knew he figured to wind up with one by bedtime, no matter what. For he'd been just too celibate for a growing boy since he'd parted with pretty Aura Lee without getting around to half the positions most gals were good sports about.

Then McArtle and McAuley came back on stage, wearing blackface with different names on the program now, as they cakewalked back and forth. A soft female voice murmured from the darkness off to his side, "That song's sort of cruel too, once you consider just how many young girls like Topsy there must have been."

Longarm wasn't surprised to see it was Vania again. He hadn't been paying attention to the minstrel song, even though he knew it as soon as he studied on it. He nodded and said, "They're stepping to it more sprightly than I suspect the composer intended. Makes no sense as a cakewalk."

But the two comical song and dance men sang it bright-eyed and bushy-tailed to a quickstep anyway, dumb as it sounded to Vania and Longarm:

> Oh, my pretty quadroon,
> My flower that faded too soon,
> My heart's like the strings on my banjo,
> All broke for my pretty quadroon!

Vania murmured, "A quadroon would be a girl who's one-quarter colored, right?"

He nodded. "Yep. Down around New Orleans they classify such matters scientifically. I don't see why, since one drop of African blood makes you a nigger socially, or even legally in some states, since President Hayes gave in on Reconstruction and let 'em pass their own laws regarding such matters."

She said, "I know. I guess the real Topsy wound up the dusky plaything of some dirty old planter."

"If she was lucky," Longarm amended, not feeling he ought to go into the probable fate of a pretty slave girl in detail. He was far more interested in who'd spoken for Vania if she was really spoken for. She seemed to speak to him one hell of a lot for a gal with another gent in mind. She was pretty, and better yet, he liked to talk to her. He just didn't need anyone else gunning for him right now. The trouble with mixing pleasure with business was that a man with a badge just never knew, for sure, who might be out to back-shoot him for what fool reason. But he knew that if he asked Vania whether or not she was free for the asking,

121

she'd think he was asking, and he had to study on that some more. For he was hurting and she was pretty, but there were others aboard as pretty, and he knew he shouldn't be fooling with any of 'em right now, cuss their soft hides and his own weak nature.

So he excused his weak self to the pretty little thing and ducked offstage completely to go back up topside. He strode the starboard cabin deck as far as the next stairwell. Once down that he found himself, as expected, on the audience side of the footlights inside. He had to get inside before that mattered. He circled around to the main entrance facing the landing. Crawfish Cartier was on duty there to deny a free show to any latecomers without tickets. He smiled at Longarm's villain makeup but asked, "Are you lost or something, Brazo? I thought Simon Legree was to enter stage right in the last act."

Longarm nodded and said, "That gives me time to determine who might have entered this way with a buffalo gun. How do I get in that limelight booth behind that jury box?"

Crawdad pointed at what looked to be a broom-closet door set sideways to the companionway leading right and left to the public seating, and said, "Tell Spotty I said it was okay. The two of you are apt to find it crowded, though."

This turned out to be the simple truth, once Longarm was up in the bitty booth with the limelight hand and the large swivel-lamp he manned.

Longarm had mixed with show folk before, so he knew how limelight worked. It was still way brighter than most any other breed of artificial light, including Mister Edison's wondrous device invented the same year as bobwire. The big hunk of lime inside the brass case didn't really burn and took ages to use up. It glowed whiter than white-hot iron as a jet of burning fuel and compressed air played against it. Then all that dazzle was concentrated into one bright beam by reflectors and lenses so the limelight hand could shine his spot of bright light most anywhere he wanted. He swung it away from the opening between him and the audience when he didn't want to spotlight anything or anybody in particular.

The hand, called Spotty for obvious reasons, was friendly enough, once Longarm explained what he was doing in there with him. By removing the floppy-brimmed black hat he wore as Simon Legree, Longarm found it easy enough to peer out the same hole without really singeing his hair on the hot brass of the swivel-lamp. At this angle he could see the audience as well as the stage, of course. But after that there was nothing much to be seen, from a lawman's point of view.

Onstage, in the center of the spot of limelight, Captain Fagan in his M.C. outfit was telling the audience what they were about to see once the first act of *Uncle Tom's Cabin* commenced. Longarm hadn't heard that part during rehearsals. Captain Fagan must not have felt the need to rehearse a piece he'd orated many a time before.

It still made Longarm feel better about the liberties they'd be taking with Miss Harriet's book. Captain Fagan saved a heap of acting, and no doubt a heap of stage scenery, by simply explaining ahead of time that the Shelby plantation had been all right before falling on hard times, but now things had gone to hell in a hack and poor old Uncle Tom had been sold down the river.

Then the curtains opened and, sure enough, all the townsfolk crowded aboard a steamboat got to stare at a smaller steamboat, or part of one leastways, and everyone seemed impressed by the prop paddle wheel, turned by hand from behind as yet another stagehand splashed water in a washtub with a shingle. Old Allan Eldrich, looking more like a forlorn darky than an English butler now, sat by the paddle box, feet dangling over the side, in the center of the limelight, lest he be mistaken for one of the other forlorn darkies on the lower deck with him. On the top deck, which was actually less than five feet above the stage but looked higher, other members of the cast milled about in modest numbers, white of skin and fancier of dress.

There was no way in hell even Sarah Bernhardt could have managed to fall in the Mississippi, or even the Missouri, through a solid pine stage. So they worked it sort of sneaky. One of the actors on the top deck wailed, "Oh, Heaven forfend, a child has fallen overboard!" just as that cuss with the basin of water splashed it good. Then Eldrich, or Uncle Tom, sprang up to dash out of sight, and the audience had to take everyone's word as they heard more splashing and a running commentary on the rescue nobody actually got to watch.

Nobody seemed to care, though. Everyone cheered and clapped or stomped when someone on stage yelled, "The darky's saved her! Got to her just as she was about to be sucked under the paddles!"

Longarm couldn't read the expressions on faces turned the other way. Most anyone in the audience was in a position to throw down on most anyone on stage, if he really had a mind to. Getting out once he'd fired a shot or more in such theatrical surroundings could be another chore entirely, as John Wilkes Booth had found out that time in Ford's Theater. Longarm decided that if he was out to assassinate Simon Legree from the audience, he'd be most likely to fire from fairly close to an exit, and then exit pronto. More gents packed guns of their own out this way than your average patron of Ford's Theater in Washington.

Figuring that much didn't serve to cheer Longarm all that much. He could only take such comfort as he could from the simple fact that nobody out to gun him could know, yet, he'd be up there in the limelight for at least a spell before this evening was over.

Thanking Spotty for the look-see, Longarm backed out of the booth and headed back to the stairwell. On the way he noticed Crawdad was no longer watching the entrance. Nobody was even watching the gangway leading ashore, for Pete's sake. Didn't they care that once the show was well under way most any asshole could just come aboard free?

He suspected they didn't as he found the stairs leading topside unguarded as well. As he mounted them he reflected that, save for a dangerous criminal now and again, most folks sneaking aboard this late were doubtless too poor to pay for a ticket and it was hardly worth anyone's time to try and sell one to such harmless simps.

He didn't like the way most anyone with a lick of nerve

could work his or her way up here and all along the cabin deck, though. Hotels half the size of this sidewheeler could get infested with sneak thieves in no time unless they had someone watching the halls better than this. When he got to the door of the cabin they'd assigned him along with his Simon Legree outfit, Longarm put a thoughtful hand inside Legree's shabby coat and tried the latch with his other. The door was still locked and seemed solid, now that one tested it for ease of entry. So he worked his way down to the backstage area. He wanted to smoke some more. He knew he couldn't. He thought he'd picked a place where he'd be out of everyone's way. But then Blanche Balmoral, coming off stage after sweetly thanking Uncle Tom for saving her sweet behind, shoved him out of her way with language Little Eva never would have used so she could change into something drier-looking. The half-drowned outfit she had on wasn't really wet. It was just made to *look* wet with some sort of tricky stretching. As he barely managed to keep from falling through some cotton bales painted on a canvas flat, Longarm was glad Little Eva got to die of an awful fever later on. It was a crying shame she didn't get run over by Apaches, real Apaches, as bitchy as she was. But he had to admit, as he watched her change duds just offstage, that few men would ever wind up torturing anyone with an ass like that, provided, of course, she wasn't one of those gals who hated screwing. He'd noticed a heap of the really bitchy ones were. He'd never figured out why the ones who liked to screw were bitchy. He'd never figured they were worth the study. Blanche caught him staring thoughtfully as she turned toward him, half done. She deliberately let a nipple show before she said, "I need someone to button this bodice up the back. Are you just going to stand there with a hard-on or would you like to give me a hand?"

He was too polite to tell her where he'd like to give her a hand, or better yet, a boot. He figured a gal that pretty was entitled to talk spiteful to men. It doubtless saved her a heap of invites to get more friendly. As he took the back of her open bodice in hand and tried to close it, he saw why she wore so little under it. He said, "No offense, Miss Blanche,

125

but I fear this childish outfit's just a size too small for your, ah, proportions."

She took a deep breath and said, "It has to be tight enough to flatten my tits, you fool. I'm supposed to be the darling daughter of a doting daddy. Would you dote on a daddy's girl with mature tits?"

He chuckled and said it would depend on whose daughter she might be. She laughed, let out all her breath, and wheezed, "Ouch! I see you're good for something, after all," as he managed to close a snap where the gap had been widest.

After that it was easy. Once he had her cinched up right she twirled around to ask him how she looked. She laughed again when he said, "Flat-chested as a ten-year-old and that flouncy skirt does a fair job hiding the true dimensions of your butt, ma'am."

She laughed again, recovered her superior expression, and told him not to get any ideas because she never indulged in affairs with other members of the troupe. He didn't ask who she *did* prefer to screw. He was a mite pissed that she seemed to think he wanted to fool with her, even though it was true.

After that, what Vania had said about being bored and anxious to go on and get it over with by the time it was his turn turned out to be ass-backwards. For events on stage seemed to be transpiring much faster than they had during rehearsals, when he hadn't had to think about anyone out in the audience with a concealed weapon.

But it was too late to back down now. So the next thing he knew he was menacing the shit out of Uncle Tom, too worried about getting shot to care whether he forgot his lines or not. So naturally, he had no trouble at all on stage as he sweat bullets every time he heard anyone out yonder cough or hiss at him for being so mean to the poor old darky who never meant no harm and only wanted a little cabin to spend his last days in with all his scattered kith and kin.

Then his part was over and he got to exit stage left, sneering, while good old George Shelby wound up to make a speech the abolitionists had sure swiped a lot of notions from in years gone by. As Longarm found a handy place to duck, he found Vania in the same slot, still made up as Topsy in blackface and thin cotton smock. In the book Little Eva and Topsy had been playmates about the same age. But Vania's Topsy was showing a mite more dusky flesh, and many more curves, than your average little colored gal, outside a house of ill repute.

He asked her what she thought of his Simon Legree. She told him. "Not bad for the first time, albeit, frankly, I thought you seemed a little stiff."

He laughed louder than she seemed to think her remark called for. Then she got it too, and fluttered her lashes to murmur, "It was you who opened my eyes to just where the part of Topsy leads to, devoid of Little Eva's generosity and Uncle Tom's influence. Do you really think I'm showing too much thigh with the skirt slit this high?"

He said, "Not too much for *my* taste. But tell me, Miss Topsy, just how far might a white gal have to go with her greasepaint to look so convincingly colored in a costume as revealing as that one?"

She dimpled demurely and replied, "You'd be able to see for yourself, if you'd like to help me remove my makeup. It's quite a chore for me alone, getting at all the, ah, awkward places with the cold cream and cotton waste dipped in witch hazel, but with just a little help from a friend . . . and seeing you're so curious about such matters. . ."

He rolled his eyes heavenward to mutter, "Well, nobody can say I made no effort at all, Lord," softly enough to make her ask just what he'd just said.

To which he replied, "Nothing. We'd best get cracking if we mean to get up to your place or mine before anyone else notices."

Chapter 16

That part was easy. It was her cabin she wanted them to wind up in, and that only made sense once he saw how much she had in the way of bottles, jars, and other ladylike crap spread out on a dressing table bigger than Billy Vail's desk back in Denver.

There were pressure lamps with thorium mantles to either side of the big mirror over the table, facing the nearby bed. But Vania told him not to light them after he'd lit the bitty wall sconce just inside the doorway leading back out on deck. She said, "I'm already having second thoughts. If I didn't have this darky makeup on you'd be able to see me blush, all over, by the little light there is in here!"

He removed his floppy black Simon Legree hat and hung it on a hook near the one lamp lit as he soberly asked what she might have on her mind to make her blush—even though he was feeling sort of blushful himself right now. He knew from past experience with gals who started out bold and wound up blushful once they were alone with a man that slowing down where the ice seemed thin was the one way to crash through to cold water for certain. So as she stood there flustered, rubbing one painted thigh against the other under that thin shimmy shirt, Longarm just reeled her in for a howdy kiss, and then sure enough, she was all over him, trying to swab his tonsils with her passionate tongue as she panted and clutched at his pants.

But when he lowered her to the bed and started to haul her cotton shift up and off her, she stopped him to moan, "No! Take me as I am right now, an amoral colored girl with no right to say no to any white man!"

He started to tell her how dumb that sounded. Then he wondered why he'd want to say a dumb thing like that, even if he wasn't really Simon Legree, the brutal abuser of folks like Topsy, male or female.

He still shucked his own duds so he could mount her halfway right at least. She had nothing on under that smooth thin shift, so her heaving breasts felt almost as naked as he liked them when he felt her moist turgid nipples against his own flushed chest. She was rolling her black-wigged head from side to side as she moaned, "Don't beat me, Massah! I'll pleasure you all you likes as long as you don't beat me with that big black whip!"

And silly as it was, it was disturbingly realistic as she got back in character with her voice as well as her greasepaint. Topsy was supposed to be young and likely still a virgin, despite her tits and the way she had those chocolate thighs wrapped around his bare waist right now. So Vania's Topsy voice was high-pitched as a young kid's as she protested, "Ooh, it's so big in my poor little pee-hole, and does this mean I ain't cherry no more, Mastah?"

He laughed and assured her he'd still respect her in the morning.

She stiffened under him and protested in a more adult tone, "That's not the way this scene goes, Brazo. You're supposed to be a dirty old white man taking advantage of a helpless colored child who doesn't know any better!"

It sure looked that way in the mirror across the way. But it felt too good to stop. So as he kept going Longarm said, "I may be dirty but I ain't that old, and abusing colored children ain't one of my usual wet dreams. But I'll be a sport and combine miscegenation with statutory rape this once, if you'll let me do it to you some more as a total-nekked white lady after you've come a time or more as Topsy in her shimmy shirt."

She clenched her jaws and groaned, "Anything you say! Just don't stop! Don't ever stop, Massah Simon! I knows some white folk say this is wicked but it feels so good!"

He had to go along with that last part, even though her little-kid voice and darky disguise were commencing to wear thin. Theatrical greasepaint wasn't made to rub off easy without removers, but between the way they were commencing to sweat and the way she thrashed about against him, he could see in the mirror he was getting sort of colored himself. It looked as if his bare hide had been smeared with shit in spots.

But what the hell, she had plenty of cold cream and witch hazel. So he kept on abusing Topsy till Vania Du Val had come more than once and confessed she couldn't take much more abuse. He knew he was sort of starting to show off as well. So he withdrew and rolled off the bed completely to rustle a smoke from the shirt he'd somehow dropped on the rug. He lit the cheroot, admiring all the brown streaks on his bare hide in her mirror, and asked her permission to do something about 'em.

She languorously indicated a big blue jar, a square glass bottle, and a pasteboard box of cotton balls as she sprawled atop her stained and rumpled bedding like one of those black golliwog dolls, tossed aside by a bored child. He could hardly wait to see her out of that crumpled shift, woolly black wig, and dusky makeup, despite the limp condition he seemed to be in right now. For he knew it would be like starting all over with another gal, and Lord only knows what sort of a voice she used, suggesting what, when she was getting laid as a white lady.

But when he suggested as much, winking at her in the mirror as he tidied himself up at her dressing table, she shook her black fuzzy wig and told him, in that same infernal Topsy voice, "Lordy Lord, Miss Vania could never do that, Massah Legree! It may be only natural for us nigger gals to carry on so shameless but . . . "

"Aw, shit," Longarm muttered, half to himself, and it didn't help when she assured him in that same dumb stage voice he could have some more of her primitive pussy if only he wouldn't talk mean to her.

He didn't talk mean to her. He could have told her that had he wanted to play kid games all night he'd have scouted up a kid. But that seemed a mite cold to say to a lady who'd likely never see thirty again, and despite the dumb way she'd gone about it, he had to allow she'd just given him a pretty good lay. So he settled for quitting with a smile while they were both still ahead.

She didn't seem to mind his not even kissing her *adios* once he had his duds back on. He'd cleaned off his Simon Legree makeup while he'd been at it, and she knew as well as he did that folks might not understand a man on deck late at night with his nose chocolate brown.

He, in turn, didn't ask when, if ever, she might want an encore. He knew it was too early for either of them to rightly say. It was only natural to want nothing more to do with a needlessly complicated lay right afterwards. He'd learned in the past not to burn bridges to Loveland behind him before he figured where he might be headed next.

Once alone on deck, he checked his watch to determine by such light as there was that it wasn't as late as he'd thought. It was barely after eleven, and by now there could be some answers to the telegram he'd sent earlier.

He didn't want to wander the streets of Sioux City dressed as old Simon Legree. So he headed for his own cabin, the one the missing actor had been using up to his mysterious disappearance, to change back into his sissy suit.

But along the way he was intercepted by a deckhand who told him Captain Fagan and some lawmen wanted him up forward in the greenroom, as show folk called a smoking lounge closed off to the general public.

Entering off the port deck, Longarm found Captain Fagan and his pilot, Crawdad, seated in one corner with a couple of well-dressed strangers. They did look sort of like lawmen, if not undertakers. Longarm had been sort of fudging on his own true identity up to now, neither lying nor volunteering to flash his badge. As he joined them he decided to play it by ear till push came to shove.

Captain Fagan said, "Brazo, these gents are with a Cincinnati insurance outfit, out our way to look into the sinking of that sternwheeler the other night."

So Longarm decided to leave his badge and identification right where they were as the taller and grayer of the pair handed him an engraved business card identifying him as one Warren Hatfield of an Ohio firm calling itself Riparian Underwriters Incorporated.

Longarm handed the card back with a friendly nod, saying, "I thought a sternwheeler with a fresh coat of paint would likely have insurance. What can I do for you, Mister Hatfield?"

The insurance dick said he could start by telling them all he knew about the accident.

Longarm saw no need to go into his own reasons for being aboard the *Prairie Rose* to begin with, or overboard when it blew up and sank. So he shrugged and said, "There's not one hell of a heap to say that you don't already know. I assume you boys have located the sunken hull and anything that's washed up so far downstream?"

Hatfield nodded grimly and replied, "We have, thanks to the marker buoy these gents were thoughtful enough to leave above the wreck. That *was* the roof of her wheelhouse you were rafting on. Her wheel and the late Captain Jacob Gilchrist have been recovered further down as well."

"What about her pilot, a somewhat truculent cuss called Turk?"

Hatfield made a wry face. "So far most of the bodies are still scraping along the bottom, however many there may be. Four women and two other men, aside from the skipper, have made it back to the surface. So we expect to recover the late Turk Mason within another day or so."

"Catfish permitting," his partner chimed in. "Folk sure look messy by the time they start to float in fresh water. Dead men seem to float facedown whilst dead women float faceup. Either way, they usually bloat so big they've busted

132

half out of their duds by the time they're found, and the *smell*—"

"Never mind all that," Hatfield said. "Mister Long, here, was about to tell us what he knew about that boiler explosion."

Longarm smiled thinly. "I was? I'd sure like to, gents. But to tell the truth I can't tell you a word more than I've already told these other gents and the landing master when we first got here, way back when. I was way back from the boilers with only one other passenger when one or more blew without warning. I called out to any other survivors, once I'd figured out what must have happened. I got no answer. Since you agree that was the top of her wheelhouse I wound up on top of, she must have blown herself to bits, mostly forward, lucky for me."

Hatfield nodded soberly. "We frankly find it amazing even *you* survived. What can you tell us about the passenger who was with you at the time of the explosion?"

Longarm said, "Nothing. He wasn't exactly with me. I just, ah, sensed his presence just before the big bang. I never got a good look at him, before or after."

Hatfield nodded. "You were obviously swimming for your life, and no doubt dazed until after you'd been aboard that rooftop for some time."

Longarm agreed that was close enough. The two of them exchanged thoughtful glances. Hatfield sighed and said, "You'd be willing to testify, of course, if you knew of anything that might have contributed to the disaster?"

His partner added, "Make that *insured* disaster. We'd be more than grateful, we'd be *generous,* if someone were to come forward and get us off the hook, if you get my meaning."

Longarm got his meaning, but kept his own feelings to himself as he replied, "I've told you all I know. I never even peeked at the innards of that steamer whilst I was aboard. How in tarnation am I supposed to account for her blowing up?"

Hatfield didn't answer. His looser-lipped sidekick said, "Turk Mason had a rep for racing and Captain Gilchrist

133

was known to be a betting man as well. There's a standard escape clause in your standard steamboat insurance policy stating that said steamboat must be operated in a safe professional manner at all times."

Longarm had known that, and the direction they were trying to steer him, early on. He didn't owe the dead skipper and pilot of the *Prairie Rose* all that much. But his old pal Gloria Grimes of the *Morning Star* had been as anxious to race as anyone and fair was fair. Had they been fellow federal agents he'd have felt honor-bound to level with them. Since they seemed to be insurance dicks out to screw the owners of the *Prairie Rose* with or without just cause, Longarm felt no call to speak ill of the dead.

But he wasn't really lying, when one studied on it, as he simply declared, "If Captain Gilchrist was racing anybody he never said so to me. Some of the other passengers were playing cards in the salon, but I don't recall any crew member making a wager with anybody about anything all the time I was aboard. Would you still like me to swear to that in court?"

They must not have. They both rose as one, but only Hatfield had the common courtesy to thank even Captain Fagan for his time.

As Fagan walked them to the stairs, outside, Crawdad Cartier cocked a brow at Longarm and said, "You're all right, Brazo. I don't care for nit-picking landlubbers neither. But just betwixt you and me and the bugs in the rug, wasn't Turk Mason going like a bat out of hell when he blowed up his boilers?"

Longarm shrugged and replied, "He was. Some closer friends of mine were steaming even faster and they *didn't* blow up. It sort of makes one wonder, don't it?"

Chapter 17

It was a balmy summer night with bugs hanging out around every street lamp, and the downtown streets of Sioux City were fairly crowded too despite the hour. Some of the Sioux City gals he passed looked mighty handsome. But naturally no lady who made love for free would be out on a public street after dark without an escort, so that was that.

Captain Fagan had said they'd be putting on a matinee and one more evening performance the following day, to steam on after skimming the ready cash of anyone in these parts at all interested in the show.

That meant Longarm could still be contacted care of the Sioux City Western Union up to, say, supper time tomorrow. Dashing this far and back after the final curtain could be cutting it too thin.

That night he wired Billy Vail where he was and where he'd be at least a spell. He brought Vail up to date on his mission. He was sort of glad they had no instructions to him from Vail. For he suspected he knew what they'd be if old Billy had cleared up that misunderstanding with the Denver P.D. by now. Knowing Billy, he'd likely had the time to pull the right strings, and with Lucky Lovelace dead, if that had been him aboard the Prairie Rose . . .

Longarm headed back for the landing, mulling over the

135

case so far as he chewed a wax match stem. He was down to chewing matches because he'd run out of cheroots. So he was watching for a tobacco shop open late too as he strode along trying to make sense out of the less-than-sensible.

He was sure the cuss who'd attacked him aboard the *Prairie Rose* had meant to drown him, not rob him, and that the cuss was now dead, whatever his name and motive.

That made sense if it had been the one and original Lucky Lovelace. What failed to make sense were the attacks on him since. For if the killer he'd been sent after had been killed . . .

"Reb Hansen was another killer entire," he muttered half aloud. "If Hansen was hired by Lovelace, the old boy I got to wrestle with aboard the *Prairie Rose* could have been a hired tough as well. Meaning Lovelace could still be alive and . . . Dumb as hell!"

For that line of reasoning only worked if a well-heeled wanted man couldn't see what he *should* have done once the *Prairie Rose* had blown up, if he'd been somewhere else at the time.

Spitting out the ragged wax match as it began to break apart between his thoughtfully gnashing teeth, Longarm muttered, "All he had to do, once it was fifty-fifty Lovelace had died in that explosion, was nothing. There's only so much time and trouble we can afford on any one case. Why let us know for certain he's still alive and at large after we had him down as likely dead down the river?"

He suddenly spied a dimly lit sign advertising tobacco products from puffing to snuffing and, sure enough, there were lamps lit in the shop below. The place was catty-corner on the far side. So Longarm stepped sideways off the high curb just as someone shot off a firecracker, or fired a gun, behind him.

Longarm had cut the other way and drawn his Webley deep in the shadows of a handy alley entrance by the time he got around to looking back the way he'd just come. There were plenty of moving targets, half of 'em swishing skirts. Anyone firing a gun up or down such a crowded walk had to be a total asshole. So Longarm put his gun away. Nobody

136

in sight seemed at all excited, and kids set off ladyfingers a month either way of the Glorious Fourth. So what the hell.

He still stayed on that side of the street, close to the cover of the storefronts, till he spied yet another tobacco shop on his side and asked the old gent in charge if he could leave by the back door once he'd bought a buck's worth of smokes.

The tobacco shop owner was a sport about that. So Longarm pissed against a fence in the dark alley as well, and made his way back to the boat landing feeling a lot better. The more he thought about it, the more likely it seemed some kid had just been acting frisky.

Back on board, after noting with a frown there was no deck watch, Longarm considered a rematch with Topsy. But while his old organ-gringer was likely up to it again, a clock tower was chiming midnight in the distance now, and the lady hadn't invited him back for second helpings.

So he headed for his own quarters instead, smoking one of his new cheroots. It was sort of pungent, even for cheap. They hadn't had his usual brand. So he leaned on the rail outside his cabin door, blowing stinky smoke rings in the moonlight a spell. He wasn't quite tired enough to pack it in for the day in the first place, and he didn't want to stink up his bitty cabin with such pungent tobacco in the second.

He decided, puffing on, that they'd put something funny in this brand of cheroots. Mayhap rosemary, anise, or both. The smoke tasted all right. It just gave off a distinct air of authority.

As if to prove he was right about them adding herbs, a female voice asked the back of his head what on earth he was smoking. He turned to see the beautiful but bitchy blonde, Blanche Balmoral, on deck in just her dressing gown and a Spanish shawl. He tried to hide his disappointment as he said he was sorry and chucked the smoke in the river below.

Blanche said, "You didn't have to do that. I never said it offended me. I just meant that tobacco smelled, ah, more like licorice or . . . oregano?"

He said, "Beats me. I just picked up some cheroots along

137

Main Street. I never asked for herbs or spices, ma'am."

She nodded and said, "They told me you'd gone into town. Frankly, I thought you'd gone somewhere else for the evening. What happened between you and our little Topsy after you left together? Didn't you want to change your luck?"

Longarm frowned down at her and softly replied, "I'm trying to keep it in mind that I am addressing a lady. You don't make that easy, Miss Blanche. For I'll be whipped with snakes if I can see what beeswax of your own it might have been had I gone here, there, or any infernal where, once I'd finished up onstage down yonder!"

She sniffed and insisted, "It is my beeswax, as you put it, whether we finish this tour professionally or not. It so happens I'm part owner of this tub as well as the star. I don't want any more love triangles disrupting the cast and crew, if that's what you want to call cats in heat fighting over the same cock!"

Longarm gulped and replied, "You sure have a delicate way of expressing your feelings, Miss Blanche. But you assured me before you ain't after any such prize, and I was given to understand both the other pretty ladies were . . . Hold on, that's right, they told me Miss Vania had herself a steady beau. Miss Blossom too."

"Did anyone tell you they'd been fighting over the same one?" asked Blanche, going on to say more venomously, "Sterling De Vere, while he lasted. I think it was Blossom who dragged him into bed first. But our Vania has had more experience at the game, as well as a nicer ass, so—"

"Hold her right there, ma'am," Longarm said, interrupting. "You may or may not be telling the truth. Whether you suffer some compulsion to spoil everyone else's fun or whether you're just a malicious gossip, Sterling De Vere would be that cuss as left your troupe before I come aboard. So why are we mean-mouthing the poor cuss? What did he ever do to you? Or is that why we're mean-mouthing him?"

Her eyes flared in the moonlight as she demanded to know just how he'd meant that last veiled remark.

He chuckled and assured her, "I wasn't out to hide my meaning, ma'am. I forget whether it was Shakespeare or some other cuss as smart who warned us all about a woman scorned, but he was on the money."

"Jesus H. Christ!" she blazed. "Do you think I had hot flashes for that effeminate twit who couldn't even remember his lines?"

Longarm shrugged and said, "I just said I wouldn't know the cuss if I caught him in bed with you or any other lady. You're the one as keeps mean-mouthing him. How come, since he's long gone and you say he never got you hot?"

She said some shocking things about Longarm and all men in general before she calmed down enough to insist, "We're too far up the river to replace either of those competitive alley cats. Vania's not a bad actress when she has her mind on her role instead of a man, and Blossom plays the piano and steam organ better than your average deckhand, as long as we can keep her broad ass planted in front of a keyboard instead of spread even broader for her latest conquest. So I want you to promise me you'll leave both of them alone."

He raised a brow. "What do I get as my treat if I do, cookies and milk or a gold star?"

"Are you referring to me, you beast?" she gasped.

Longarm had really meant one of those gilt-paper stars they gave good little boys in school, as a matter of fact, but since she seemed out to put a double meaning to everything, and since she was a star with fairly golden curls, he had to laugh sort of dirty.

He laughed again when the bitchy blonde slapped his face and turned on one heel to flounce back to her own lonesome bed around the bend. For she hadn't hit hard enough to matter.

It was up for grabs whether she'd been afraid of hurting his jaw or her hand. He didn't feel like starting another pungent smoke. So he ducked into his own cabin, shut the jalousie door, and undressed by the meager moonlight coming through the slats.

He took his time, hanging things up for a change. That was one of the bad things about wearing nice duds. It

139

inspired a man to prissy habits. As he turned the covers down and slid into bed, bare-ass, there came a discreet tap-tapping on the door and someone rattled the latch, pleading, "Hurry! I don't want to be seen!" in a breathless whisper.

So Longarm did what most any proper gent would have done under the circumstances. He let her in, rebolted the door after her, and got a good hold on her in the dark, whispering, "I was sort of hoping you'd be back." He kissed her hard and lowered her gently to the bed, running his free hand down her silk-covered curves as she giggled and whispered, "You don't waste time, do you? How come you were expecting me? I thought I was acting pretty prim and proper out on deck."

He kissed her again and assured her, "You surely were. To the casual eye we could have been dedicated enemies. But as long as we're going to be pals now . . . "

"Wait!" she insisted, even as his questing fingers got the front of her dressing gown open enough to make him wonder how blond she might be down yonder.

"We have to agree to some rules regarding my reputation," she insisted. "Stop that, you silly, this is serious. If I give in to you tonight you won't tell the whole world in the morning, will you?"

He began to massage her slit skillfully as he assured her he wouldn't even tell a fly on the wall. She might have had some other demands in mind, but by now he could tell from the way he had her gushing that this was no time for idle chatter. So he just parted her gown all the way out of the way and she parted her thighs for him as the Red Sea had parted for Moses, albeit her warm depths felt somewhat tighter than any fool sea as he entered her, glad to discover she was a mite tighter than old Vania rather than the other way around.

For he'd had time to rest his back and replenish his amorous ammunition, but he still wished he was starting fresh with something this swell. He penetrated her deep as he could, and then reached down to clasp one of her buttocks in each palm in hopes of keeping it up as well as all the way

140

in. That was when he first noticed what a truly big behind she had, delicate as she was everywhere else. He laughed like hell as he compared what he had in hand with what he'd seen the time he'd watched Blanche change her duds. When the somewhat broader gal in hand asked what was so funny, he gallantly replied, "Nothing, Miss Blossom. I mean to screw you serious as hell, you sassy little thing!"

Chapter 18

So he did and, next morning, neither the imaginative Vania nor the broad-assed Blossom let on butter would have melted in their pretty mouths, albeit the bitchy Blanche kept staring at all three of them suspiciously.

They put on their matinee show without incident, save that Blanche complained Longarm's Simon Legree was stiff and not sneery enough.

Afterwards he went over to the Western Union to learn that sure enough Billy Vail had invited the Denver police commissioner to a sit-down dinner and so all was forgiven. Mrs. Vail sure cooked swell grub, and Billy served good liquor with a generous hand when he was of a mind to please.

But even though Longarm was invited to head home now, since Vail agreed that had likely been Lucky Lovelace he'd drowned a few nights back, Longarm wired back that he meant to check out that tip about the killer being spotted aboard the *Morning Star*, seeing that he was on the same river and knew the more honest folks aboard that other sternwheeler. Then he added:

WHAT ABOUT POSSIBLE ABDUCTION AURA LEE QUESTION MARK SHE SAID SHE WAS AFTER HENDERSON NOT ELOPING WITH HIM STOP

He didn't bother to sign it, since that would have cost at least another nickel and who else would be wiring anything like that?

Captain Fagan hadn't said for certain where they'd put in next for exactly how long. Showboats preferred towns along the river where a heap of folks had no handier entertainment. It followed that neither a one-horse town with too tiny a population or a bigger town with a slew of first-class theaters was good for showboats. That was how come they'd played Council Bluffs, across from Omaha, instead of Omaha itself.

He found this out from Vania when she waylaid him in his own quarters after he got back from town. He was glad to see he'd been right in assuming it would be like starting up fresh with another gal completely, once he had her taking it dog-style in the buff with neither that woolly wig nor darky makeup on. The only trouble was that now she wanted him to pretend he was a wild stallion and that she was a runaway mare in heat. He said it might be more fun if she'd be Jeannie with the Light Brown Hair. But she said she didn't get half as excited to Stephen Foster ballads. So that inspired him to roll her on her back and treat her to a soft rendition of "Riley's Daughter" with two pillows under her rump, and that worked pretty good.

Vania seemed to enjoy the part of Riley's Daughter as they went jig-a-jig-jig indeed. For despite her stage name she knew what jig meant in Gaelic. So the next thing he knew she was on top, talking dirty as hell in a thick Irish brogue as she warned him of the murtherous consequences if ever her cruel father, the notorious One-Ball Riley, ever found out she'd been doing this balls and all.

He didn't mind until she tried to get his balls in too. He protested, "That won't work, as well you must know, since every growing boy tries that at least once with anyone half so willing."

So she found something even more wicked to do to his privates, with her sassy mouth, as he lay back to just enjoy it, softly singing:

Came a knock upon me doorstep,
Who should it be but One-Ball Riley,
Two horse pistols in his hands,
Looking for the man who shagged his daughter!
Tiddy I yee, tiddy I yo,
Tiddy I yee for One-Ball Riley,
Jig-a-jig-jig, balls and all,
Rub-a-dub-dub shag on!

To which she replied, moving to spit herself on his newly inspired shaft:

Now as he goes walking down the shtreet,
The paple from their doorsteps holler.
There goes that Protestant son of a bitch!
The one who shagged the Riley's daughter!

And if the rhyme was a mite off she had the meter just right. So who cared? But in the end, she couldn't say for certain where they'd be stopping next.

So they stopped what they were doing and split up to catch some rest before supper and the evening show.

They had baked beans and Vienna sausage for supper. The evening show went better than the matinee, to Longarm's way of thinking. But once again their bitchy star, in blackface as Eliza at the end, reviled his portrayal of Simon Legree.

He could only reply he'd never been a slave driver before, and suggest she could likely use some abuse from him as long as she was still in character as a slave gal.

She didn't seem to think that was funny, and it was getting tedious to get slapped by such a silly bitch. So he grabbed her wrist this time and she gasped, "Oh! You're hurting me, you brute!"

So he told her with a villainous laugh, "I'm just trying to get into my part. What do you reckon I'd have really done to you if you hadn't escaped across the ice from me and my bloodhounds just now?"

She twisted away and flounced out of sight. Captain Fagan must have been watching from some favorite ambush amid the scenery flats. For he was suddenly there, murmuring, "Take it easy on the girl, son. We'd be in a fine mess if she left the cast on us this far from civilization!"

Longarm said, "I've been trying to steer clear of her. She keeps coming around to beat me up for some mysterious reason."

Captain Fagan sighed and said, "Her reasons aren't that mysterious. As to her remarks about your acting abilities, she has a point. No offense, Brazo, but I've seen more convincing villains in my time."

Longarm protested, "I never told you I was a villain, or even an actor, damn it. Get somebody else to play Simon Legree if you want to. I don't enjoy getting hissed at to begin with."

Fagan sighed and muttered, "Don't tempt me. It'd mean shifting parts around until we might wind up with you as Little Eva. Of course, in a pinch, both Drew and Redfern have played Legree in their time. Hasn't everybody? But we'd better stick with things the way they are for now."

Longarm replied he wasn't the one doing all the bitching, and added, "I don't even know where I'll be getting hissed at next. Is it supposed to be a secret where we're heading tonight?"

Fagan shook his head. "Yankton, Lord willing and the river doesn't drop another mark under us. It'll take us longer than overnight to make Yankton, though. She's around sixty miles upstream as the crow might fly, and more like a hundred as the river winds, the twisty son of a bitch."

Longarm nodded. "I figured it might be Yankton. Nothing betwixt here and there save for stock spreads, Indian agencies, and thin-spread nesters, right?"

Fagan said, "So far. Give the country a chance to fill out a bit and this river will be another Nile or Yangtze!"

Longarm resisted the temptation to inquire how that might be considered an improvement. Looking on the brighter side, Yankton was the current capital of the Dakota Territory. So there'd be not only a Western Union there but plenty of backup and handy river-to-rail connections if he needed 'em.

He didn't see how he'd need 'em, unless he figured out what in thunder was going on, though. So he didn't do or say a thing to discourage Captain Fagan from scouting up his engineer and pilot to get the show on the road or, in this case, the river.

His afternoon session in the sack with Vania before all that fussing and cussing on stage had left Longarm a mite spent. So even though he'd recovered his wind by the time the showboat shoved off, he sort of hoped old Vania had had enough, or that she'd at least settle for some simple down-home screwing if she wanted more by moonlight. For all that playacting she demanded along with the bumps and grinds took as much out of a man as the bumps and grinds. It was tough to screw passionately while you were trying not to laugh, lest you bust the spell and freeze her in mid-motion at a mighty awkward moment.

But after smoking out on deck alone a spell, he figured Vania had decided to have mercy on him. So he decided to quit while he was ahead. They all had a long day ahead of them at the rate this tub was moving.

Had it been darker one might have thought they were tearing up the river at a dozen knots. But since Crawfish had wisely waited for plenty of moonlight, one could see that despite the splashing and thrashing of the side paddles they were barely moving in relation to the window lights on shore. The current above Sioux City was pushing them backwards almost as fast as the high-pressure boilers and giant paddle wheels could push them the other way.

High-pressure boilers were something to think about as one got ready for bed aboard a steamboat bucking the Big Muddy. Old James Watt, who'd invented the modern steam engine, had gone to his grave convinced modest steam pressure was the only way to go. But the whippersnappers who'd taken over after Watt's original patents ran out had argued Watt's low-pressure notions were wasteful of fuel as well as slow. So they'd started to raise the pressure, first to alarming and then to suicidal levels in the view

146

of the original steamfitters. The safety valve was supposed to be the answer, and most of the time it was. James Watt had been right about boiler plates having inevitable flaws you'd never notice till you strained things past a point of no return. So the safety valve atop the steam dome was designed to give way before anything else, in a way that did no damage.

There was little more to a safety valve than a powerful coil spring holding a tapered plug in a reamed-out hole in the steam dome, much as that little Dutch boy had held his finger in the dike.

Safety valves were rated to the safe operating pressure of a particular steam plant. You'd want a way stiffer valve for a steamboat than a rail locomotive, and neither could have run on the operating pressure of a farmer's threshing machine. The fact that steamboats blew up way more often than threshing machines or even steam locomotives reflected on the fact that river pilots, faced with hard choices, tended to run their engines at higher pressure to begin with, and when that didn't work, try for more, illegally as well as foolishly.

But neither Crawdad Cartier nor Curly Garth looked like assholes, and it was safe to assume nobody was about to wire any safety valves shut so *Fagan's Floating Follies* could move a mite faster or blow up. Longarm got rid of his last smoke and ducked into his cabin, to find that while old Vania had had enough, Blossom Bascom hadn't. So what could one say to a naked lady in one's bed but "howdy," and what could one do to her there but try.

Blossom did her best to please him as well. There was a lot to be said for an almost painfully tight tunnel of love beyond a welcome of marshmallow-soft quivering flesh. But then she put a damper on it by demanding while she was on top, with a cruel advantage, that he "promee-womee" to love her and nobody else but her for as long as the rivers should run, the grass should grow, and so on.

He said he'd study on it. (No man born of mortal woman was about to say no while he was coming.) But even as he was ejaculating straight up into her delightfully bouncing body, he began to find the disappearance of the handsome Sterling De Vere less mysterious.

The bitchy but likely accurate Blanche Balmoral had told him the missing actor had been dallying with both this one and the even wilder Vania. Or had it been vice versa? In either case, as they were sharing a smoke afterwards, he snuggled her soft nude body closer to his and confided, "I get along better than most with Indians because I never make promises about rivers running and grass growing. It's pure bull that George Washington ever said anything like that to any Indian, by the way. Old George didn't like Indians well enough to promise 'em anything, having served under Braddock in the French and Indian Wars. That ambush they marched into on the trail to Fort Duquesne was way messier than Little Big Horn, by the way. Only Washington and a few others managed to fight their way out with all their hair."

She took a drag on their cheroot and asked what possible connection there could be between their undying love and dead generals.

He said, "Digression is the mark of a man with something awkward to say. But since you ask, I don't make deals I don't intend to keep. I can promise you I'll be traveling with this showboat as far as Yankton because there's no place closer I can get off, dry. I might or might not be going on with you all after that. It all depends on what happens in Yankton. Meanwhile, we're here together, and as soon as I get my breath back I mean to make love to you some more. If this be treason, make the most of it. Give me liberty or go find somebody else."

She protested, "I don't want anyone else, Patrick Henry. Can't you even promise to be mine, all mine, as long as you're aboard this showboat? I was so afraid that other mean thing would get you first and—"

"Are we talking about Miss Blanche Balmoral?" he asked, interrupting, knowing they likely weren't. "She ain't my type."

Blossom giggled and replied, "That's for certain." She began to toy with the hairs on his belly, confiding, "If the truth be known, she'd rather screw me than you. She's one of those lizzy gals our mothers warned us about. Couldn't you tell?"

Longarm laughed incredulously and demanded, "How? I ain't even sure what lesbians *do* with the gender they prefer! You say she can screw another gal? No offense, but I just don't see how or, ah, how you'd know if she could."

Blossom ran her soft fingers further down his belly as she shyly murmured, "She has this mighty clever invention made out of pink India rubber, and as to the very few times I let her, ah, show it to me, a healthy young woman has needs and one can't just satisfy them with members of the hoi polloi."

He said, "I've read what Miss Virginia Woodhull has to say about Free Love and the practical advantages of bisexual friendships betwixt emancipated females. But tell me something, might Miss Vania be on the same terms with the prima donna of this here showboat?"

Blossom began to fondle him more freshly as if inspired by the discussion of forbidden fruit. She said, "Good heavens, Vania can convince herself she's a naughty colored girl or Joan of Arc getting raped by Englishmen in armor if she puts her mind to it. Lord knows what she and Blanche were up to before I came aboard down the river. But she told me one time, when we were on friendlier terms, that she really liked boys best, the same as me."

She proved that to Longarm's satisfaction by rolling on to her hands and knees to lower her rosebud lips to the wonders she'd already wrought with her soft skilled hand. He knew she couldn't answer with her mouth full, and in any case he could guess at how the rest of it went. So it was small wonder Blanche Balmoral was bitching him. She'd no doubt been bitching that other poor cuss, De Vere, till he'd had enough of a three-way feud between a lesbian and two less particular sex fiends. The poor bastard must have felt lucky to escape with his life. Assuming he had.

That was something to study on, as soon as one studied on it.

Chapter 19

Daybreak found Longarm alone in his mighty rumpled bedding and *Fagan's Floating Follies* still doing her damnedest to get to Yankton sometime that day. Longarm tidied up, got dressed, and stepped out on deck to see the Big Muddy was living up to its nickname and then some. The level of the upper Missouri was lower, swifter, and looked more like hot chocolate about to boil over than anything one might to dip a paddle in. So the paddles were churning like hell, throwing thick chocolate back down the river as they tried to shove the showboat up it. They were making progress, but old Crawdad up in the wheelhouse still had his morning chores cut out for him as they wound their way up the main channel.

It took one hell of a pilot to determine which trickle of liquid mud the main channel might be. The upper reaches of the river were "braided" as the mapmakers described any streambed that was part streams and part sandbars separating the interlacing water. A craft this size needed at least four feet of water to float her, running light. From the amount of freshly exposed muddy sand all about, they'd be lucky to make it much beyond Yankton. Say Fort Pierre at best. Pushing as far up as Milk River was out of the question, and if little Captain Gloria Grimes hadn't turned her *Morning Star* around by now, she figured to ground somewhere the far side of Standing Rock, shallow-draft as the smaller sternwheeler might be.

But first things coming first, Longarm went aft to see what they were serving for breakfast. The kitchen was serving all the flapjacks and pork sausages a sensible soul might want. From where she held court at one end of the table, Blanche Balmoral was serving more dirty looks than Longarm felt the situation warranted, since she'd already assured him she didn't want any slap-and-tickle with him.

Neither Vania nor Blossom let on they'd ever heard tell of such fun with anyone as they demurely stuffed their pretty faces, not looking up from their coffee and grub. So after a time the bitchy blonde left the table with a toss of her artificial curls, and only Blossom looked up to catch Longarm's eye, dimple slightly, and go back to staring intently at her half-finished second helping. He noticed Vania ate more discreetly. That no doubt accounted for her more elfin ass, bless both their varied asses.

After a second cup of strong black coffee Longarm excused himself so he could smoke one of his nice-tasting but odd-smelling cheroots on deck. With both his innards and privates well sated for the moment, he found the morning air invigorating. So he strode up forward to watch as Crawdad skillfully swung the bow port or starboard in a manner Longarm found surprising at times as well as interesting. For while he knew a mite more about running a river than your average barber or house painter, he still guessed wrong, now and again, when the unseen pilot up above him chose what appeared to be the lesser of two channels.

To either side of the wide braided riverbed the shores rose high as a storm-tossed sea of grass, gone tawny as the hide of a monstrous muscular lion under the searing summer sun of the High Plains.

For a good part of the morning that was all there was to see. But before noon they'd passed some pensive-looking Indians watching from a rise, and one time Crawdad spooked a handful of buffalo with his steam whistle. But it was after they'd served noon dinner, chicken and dumplings with rhubarb pie, when they began to pass sod houses and fenced-in quarter-sections, with little ragged-ass kids waving from most every fence line, as Crawdad favored 'em with polite but economical toots. For even though the boat seemed to be approaching civilization and a place to put in, they were fighting the Big Muddy every yard of the way at full steam ahead, meaning the pressure in the boilers would be a tad low no matter how hot the flames were roaring under the boilers.

Longarm hoped old Curly was as good an engineer as Crawdad was a pilot. For Gloria Grimes had told him, that other time, how easy it was to get in trouble with the engines using steam as fast as or faster than your fire could boil water.

It was sudden stops that could make any pilot glad he had a good safety valve. For should he suddenly have to shut his steam throttle for any reason, the roaring flames could flash more water into steam than anyone with a lick of sense really needed or wanted, with no place to go but out the safety valve.

But what the hell, they doubtless had all the safety valves they needed, and in any case the twin paddle wheels were demanding more pressure than poor Curly had to offer.

Longarm knew he was right when, once more alone in the bow, he noticed they were passing some small waving kids without even a cricket chirp from their steam whistle. So he took off his sporty straw hat and waved it like hell, hoping they could see him in the shadows by the silent calliope behind him.

He was waving at another bunch of nester kids and their worn-looking mule when Blossom joined him, smiling mighty innocently for a gal who gave such great French lessons in private, and asked him how soon they'd reach Yankton.

He told her it couldn't be too far, seeing most nesters liked to settle within an easy drive to the nearest town whenever such public land was thrown open to settlement. So when she saw they were nearing a good-sized cluster of rooftops and a steeple up ahead, she plunked her friendly broad butt down at the calliope and turned it on to rattle any windows for at least a mile with "Marching through Georgia."

That was likely safe enough to play this far north, this long after anyone had really marched through Georgia, but Longarm knew more about steam engines than she did. So he warned her she was stealing power from their paddle wheels, or at least he tried to. She couldn't hear anything softer than the report of, say, a .45 above all the racket she was making. He was about to stride over and shake her when he got shook, hard, the other way, and in the confusion that followed, the only thing he was certain of was that they were hard aground.

Then he noticed the calliope pipes go up an octave and change in pitch. They sounded awful. But when Curly Garth came around the bend with blood in his eye to demand she stop, Longarm darted between them to shout, "No! We want her to open all stops, not shut a damned one!" And when that didn't work, he had to deck Curly with a left-cross sucker punch and quickly flatten both hands on the keyboard next to Blossom's just as she tried to stop marching through Georgia, bewildered by the way her steam organ was acting up. As she stared at him thundergasted, Longarm put his mouth to her ear to shout, above the banshee wailing of his own efforts at the keyboard, "Open some valves! Any damn valves! We have to bleed a runaway boiler through this fortunate musical instrument!"

She understood what he wanted, but her calliope didn't work that way. So the best she could manage was a mighty classical exercise, played with all fingers of both hands while the bass keys he held down droned on. They sounded mighty dreary, between the two of 'em.

Off to one side, where he'd landed, the burly Curly looked more astounded than angry as he got back to his feet, staring saucer-eyed at them. Longarm didn't want to have to shoot him, so he yelled "Safety valve!" over and over until Curly read his lips the right way, yelled something back, and vanished from view.

By this time half the others on board had come forward to stare in wonder at the two obvious lunatics playing a mad duet on the steam calliope. Captain Fagan came down from the wheelhouse, trying to yell something about needing power to back off a damned bar, as Longarm read his irate lips.

But the two of them kept the calliope screaming as if their lives depended upon it, knowing it did, until suddenly the sounds subsided with bubbling whimpers and Longarm announced, in the sudden din of silence, "It looks like we saved the day. Nice playing, pard. Was that Beethoven or Bach we were playing just then?"

Blossom laughed weakly and replied, "I don't know about you but I was trying for *Götterdämmerung* by Wagner."

Captain Fagan said, "It sure was the gawddamnedest noise I ever hear coming outten that calliope! Would somebody care to tell me why, gawddamn it?"

Longarm started to explain, but even as he rose Curly Garth came back, packing a pipe wrench and an enraged expression as he yelled, "Bailing wire! Some stupid suicidal son of a bitch wrapped at least a dozen yards of bailing wire betwixt the coils of our safety-valve spring! I don't see how in tarnation we're going to get it out, now that the wire's been squoze so tight by the valve trying to open a lot!"

There was a worried murmur from the actors and crew members. Some of them even understood what Curly was talking about. Old Allan Eldrich said, "Good Lord! Someone must have wanted all of us blown higher than the sky!"

Longarm said, "I ain't sure anything's higher than the sky but we'd have surely had a boiler explosion, just now, if Miss Blossom hadn't been seated at her calliope. That was all that relieved the pressure when the pilot shut the throttle topside!"

Captain Fagan said, "Crawdad wants to back-water the paddles now. You say there's no way, Curly?"

The engineer said, "There's a way. We can screw the bad valve back in place for now, and rig this calliope to bleed pressure by unshipping, say, an octave of pipes and pounding corks from the kitchen into 'em."

Blossom opined that was a mighty mean way to treat a musical instrument. Longarm told her, "It's still a smart notion. Each pipe is a mite wider, moving down the scale. So, given about the same size cork stoppers driven in to each, with more or less effort, they ought to blow one at a time, if they blow, almost as smooth as a safety valve would open. You see, you can't let it all out or hold it all in, so—"

"Never mind all that!" Captain Fagan shouted. "What I want to know is who did such a dirty deed in the first damn place! The monster must have been out to murder us all!"

Longarm nodded and said, "That lets most everyone here off our list of likely suspects, Captain. The culprit snuck into the engine room last night in Sioux City, most likely during the show when nobody would have been watching. It would have taken some time to wrap all that wire around the valve and—"

"In the dark, way up high," Blanche Balmoral said, interrupting, her voice dripping honey and acid as she added, "Meaning a tall man who knew his way about below."

Captain Fagan scowled and said, "We've plenty of tall gents who know their way about the boat, Miss Blanche. But as Brazo just said, the rascal who rigged that boiler to blow would have had to be out of his mind to stay aboard and steam on with his intended victims!"

"Or a good swimmer," countered the bitch blonde, staring right at Longarm as she purred, "I never intimated the deed was done by any member of our regular cast and crew. None of *them* were ever aboard *another* steamboat when it blew up, killing everyone but one sole survivor on one oddly handy escape raft."

Longarm knew why everyone was staring his way now. It sounded a mite suspicious to *him*, and he knew for a fact she was full of it.

He snorted in disgust and said, "That sure explains why I just saved us all, with the help of Miss Blossom and Curly. Some gents collect stamps whilst others blow up steamboats for a hobby."

He saw he'd scored a point with Captain Fagan. Then Blanche said, "*Somebody* just tried to kill us all. He'd know

155

better than the rest of us why he'd want us or the folks on that *other* steamboat dead."

Longarm stared soberly at Captain Fagan to demand, "Do you think anyone here wired that boiler to blow, sir?"

Fagan sighed uncertainly and replied, "Of course not. But just the same, you might start looking for another way up the river once we reach Yankton. It's nothing personal but, as Miss Blanche here says, your acting isn't quite convincing enough."

Chapter 20

Things might have gone worse. Had anyone made any definite charges when they finally limped in to Yankton that afternoon, Longarm would have had to show his badge and credentials. Besides, the big sidewheeler wasn't going to make it much farther up the river with the water this low in any case.

He had no baggage, and parting was more a pain in the ass than a sweet sorrow to a tumbleweed man like him. So he would have simply strode ashore without looking back. But Captain Fagan stopped him near the gangway, holding out a modest wad of silver certificates as he said, "We owe you for two turns on stage as a feature performer, and your Simon Legree wasn't all that bad, but what can I say? She's a part owner as well as the star."

Longarm was tempted to tell Fagan to shove the damned money where the sun never shone. But such self-destructive pride was for bullfighters and bitchy blondes. So he took the money, knowing it would do him more good in his pocket than up Fagan's ass.

As they shook on it, Longarm sheepishly allowed, "You warned me she was nursing odd worries. You might have put things stronger. Did you have to put that other horny cuss, De Vere, ashore, or was it his own grand notion?"

Fagan sighed and said, "A little of both. I was looking to replace him with someone ugly or queer. But you've no doubt noticed how many theatrical booking agents there are along the Missouri."

Longarm laughed, let go, and they parted friendly.

The modest-sized city of Yankton, along the north bank of the river, which trended westward in these parts, had grown in about twenty years from a trading post catering to the Yankton bands of the so-called Sioux to the current capital of Dakota Territory, organized as such back in '61 after the Sioux got too frisky under Little Crow for Washington to worry about earlier treaties.

Whether this had been right or wrong, there was both a Western Union and a U.S. marshal's office here in Yankton. So Longarm went first to see if Billy Vail had wired any further facts or at least some damned instructions. But they had nothing for him at Western Union, likely because nobody in Denver knew exactly where he was and Billy Vail thought a nickel a word was too steep unless he had something important to say.

Longarm rectified that by wiring where he was and how come. Then, as long as he was there and had no idea when he'd ever get out of Yankton, he sent queries to others who had to know a heap more than he did right now. For until he knew more about the safety valve of that demolished sternwheeler, and had a head count on just how many others on board had really drowned or only wound up "missing," he had too many likely suspects, with likely motives, to keep straight in his head.

He said as much, a few minutes later, when he paid a courtesy call on the local federal law in the person of Marshal Maxwell Cox, who knew Billy Vail of old, knew Longarm by rep, and didn't seem to give a gnat's fart about the puzzle Longarm was trying to solve, once the younger lawman had explained it to him in the saloon across the way from the frame federal building.

They'd taken a pitcher of beer to a corner table in deference to old Maxwell's dignity and game leg. He claimed he still had an arrowhead, a flint one, embedded too deep to be worth all the fuss and gore. He said he'd heard about the *Prairie Rose* blowing up down the far side of Sioux City, but that he frankly hadn't been following up on the sad story.

Sipping some suds, he confided, "If bodies or even wreckage floated upstream instead of downstream, or if one human soul in Dakota Territory had even heard the explosion, we might have had to file a fool report. You know how they are back East. But as far as I hear tell, none of the folk killed down betwixt Iowa and Nebraska had kith or kin in these parts."

"Wouldn't the *Prairie Rose* have steamed through a heap of Dakota if she hadn't blown up?" asked Longarm.

The crusty old Cox shrugged and said, "Sure. The Big Muddy swings north just past Springfield Bend, and don't swing west no more till Garrison. It's still running through Dakota Territory as far west as its junction with the Yellowstone. After that it's Montana's damn problem. That's likely where most of them drownded passengers were headed, now that they've struck so much color over yonder. What do you expect me and my boys to do about folks from other parts drowning in other parts, old son?"

Longarm insisted, "Lucky Lovelace was a federal want, accused of gunning our own, Marshal."

Cox sipped, shrugged, and said, "You say he was likely the one as went swimming with you just before the *Prairie Rose* blew sky high. I see no reason to doubt you. Now give me a reason why any of us ought to be really concerned with recovering his corpse."

Cox sipped more suds, burped, and added, "For all we know it's *been* recovered. Stiffs have gone halfway down to Saint Lou, and since you can't say for certain which of the men on the passenger list might have jumped you that night . . . "

"I can't even say for *uncertain*," Longarm noted with a sigh, repeating, "I never got a good look or a good grip on the son of a bitch. I know he was wearing pants and built less romantic than the average female I've wrestled with in my time."

Marshal Cox poured more beer in his stein as he said, "My point exactsome. Whatever he looked like, he paid for his crime with his life, and there's no way to wrap things tighter than with a dead man, untidy as that may sound."

Longarm made a wry face and said, "It sounds downright sloppy. We can't even say for sure what crimes he had in mind. If that attempt to shove me over the side and under the paddles had been the end of it, I'd feel free to write it off as a last fatal bid on the part of a fleeing felon who'd figured my identity and feared I'd figured his. But if I went swimming with Lucky Lovelace, and he drowned, who's been trying to kill me since, and why?"

Cox swallowed, thought, and suggested, "Revenge? Makes no sense for Lovelace to make you suspect he's still alive if he's really alive."

Longarm nodded. "I'd have written him off as dead and stopped hunting him after coming out the sole survivor of that big bang, if only that had been the end of the banging. But betwixt the way guns keep going off and steam boilers keep blowing up . . ."

"You don't know the explosion of the *Prairie Rose* was an attempt on your life, or even deliberate," the older lawman observed.

To which Longarm could only reply with a sheepish smile, "You're right. I could be playing chess when the name of the game's really checkers. Starting with the mystery man as pushed me over the rail just in time, bless his black heart. He'd have never been aboard at the time if he'd known the tub was about to blow up under us both. Let's just say an overly ambitious pilot and reckless engineer took one chance too many with steam pressure and that that part was really the accident it appeared. That would allow Lovelace or a confederate the motive and opportunity to roll over the rail with me and drown. But someone for certain rigged that showboat to blow up under me, after failing to kill me, more than once, on shore!"

Cox suppressed a yawn and said, "We got the wired bulletin on that hired gun you shot it out with. So now we can forget him too."

"Not the sneak or sneaks he was working for," Longarm said, leaving his own drained stein the way it was. "Someone took a shot at me, mayhap two shots, after I'd already downed their hired gun. Then someone slipped aboard the showboat, likely during the show, and wired that safety valve stuck to kill me more certain later on. The murderous bastard must have known we'd be bucking the current with the fires hot as old Curly and his black gang could manage. The only thing that saved us when we hit that sandbar and all that pressure built up in seconds with nowhere to go was that providential pipe organ. The cuss with the big roll of hay wire must know more about steamboats in general than showboats in particular."

Cox poured the last of the beer, asking, "If it was you he was after, how come he had to kill you so scientifical? You told me on the way over here that you'd been up on stage in front of God and everybody whilst someone fooled about in the boiler room. What was there to stop him from just blowing you away as you was beating on Uncle Tom, you villainous cuss?"

"Stage costume and makeup," said Longarm without hesitation. He saw Marshal Cox knew less about show boats than he did, now, and explained, "I wasn't alone up yonder. They had me in a floppy-brimmed hat as might have made my face tough enough to recognize *without* the bushy brows, hollow cheeks, and green jaws as goes with the part. I wasn't even wearing these same pants. As for the other white men on stage in blackface—"

"I'd have tried to blow you up too," Marshal Cox said, interrupting. "That's assuming I was a really murderous son of a bitch, of course. They must want you bad, or just not give a shit about the lives of even pretty human beings!"

Longarm nodded soberly. "I figure it's both. Someone ruthless as a Comanche horse thief wants me dead, bad enough to pay professional killers to do the dirty deed, dirty as it takes. So all I have to figure is who'd have that good a reason to have me killed."

Cox nodded. "I'd best get back to my desk across the way, Longarm. Tell Billy I asked about him. Where might you be headed next, in case anyone asks?"

As they both got to their feet Longarm replied, "On up the river, soon as I figure how. As wild a shot as that one tip offers, I may as well make certain Lucky Lovelace didn't get off the *Morning Star* in the headwaters mining country."

"What about your friends aboard that showboat?" asked Cox as they both headed out to the sunny street.

Longarm said, "They ain't my friends no more. They ain't even in danger now that I ain't with 'em. If the mastermind behind all this skullduggery has anyone here in Yankton, he must know by now that I'm safe ashore—or ashore leastways."

Out on the walk Marshal Cox asked, "What if they try for you some more?"

To which Longarm could only reply, "I'm banking on it. It's the only way I'm likely to catch anybody, since I've no notion at all who I might be after!"

Chapter 21

They were talking about building a college in Yankton, but as yet there wasn't all that much to see, and whatever the reason some slippery son of a bitch had for killing him, Longarm didn't see how this godforsaken river port could have all that much to do with it.

Meanwhile, at the railroad depot, they'd told him he could get as far upstream as Milk River by rail if he'd like to wait a spell and then change trains, more than once, with one such transfer involving an overnight layover. So he headed for a saloon overlooking the boat landing in hopes of a better suggestion.

But it only took him a needled beer and half a cheroot at the bar with a generally friendly riverboat crowd to learn he'd find few craft headed upstream at all, and none at all as far as Milk River. For despite the break in the long drought the High Plains had suffered through most of the '70's, the river was way down for this time of the year and figuring to fall further.

"It's the infernal sodbusting nesters!" a regular who looked more cow than river grumbled. "Stands to reason exposing all that soil to the sun and wind has to dry the land out intolerable. The dry dirt sucks water outten the river the way blotting paper sucks up ink. We never had low water this early in the summer when this territory was all under six inches of sod, even in a dry year!"

There was a grumble of agreement along the bar. Longarm just sipped more suds. He'd heard that theory before. He didn't know if there was anything to it or not. It was true those heavy John Deere plows turned dark moist soil on the first pass, even in August, where the prairie had never been tilled before. It was just as true forty acres turned over and drilled to barley could be bone-dry and wind-blowing before your barley came up, while corn was usually a waste of effort west of say longitude 100 on buffalo range Wakan Tonka had never intended for such thirsty crops.

Longarm suspected it would take far more plowing than he'd seen so far to alter the water table under the High Plains enough to notice, and in any case the only thing that really mattered was low water, no matter what the reason.

Since it seemed he had the choice of chasing a will-o'-the-wisp the tedious way or packing it in and heading back to Denver, Longarm ordered another beer. He had to study before he made either disgusting move. For he knew that no matter which he made, he'd likely wind up wishing he'd made the other.

Then Curly Garth came in with a gent in bib overalls Longarm had never seen before. The engineer of the showboat spied Longarm about the same time and came over, wary-eyed but holding out his paw polite enough. As they shook, Curly said, "Brazo, this here's Red Woods. Just sold us a new safety valve and helped install it. I, ah, tried to warn you both them gals was spoken for."

Longarm shook with Red as well, noting he was really gray, and turned back to Curly. "You did indeed, albeit I got the fool notion the competition was with other males."

Then he signaled the barkeep, adding, "Let's not cry over spilt milk when the suds they serve here are so refreshing. I'm way more interested in that safety valve you just had to replace than the odd romances aboard that showboat."

As Longarm ordered a round for the three of them, Curly confided that Red Woods was a licensed steamfitter who knew about such matters and then some.

164

Longarm said, "*Bueno*. I'd best tell both you boys that I'm the law, federal, because I'm about to get nosey as hell about your own beeswax and some of my questions may sound odd, coming from a casual drinker."

Curly blinked, laughed, and said, "Hot damn, I knew from the first you were covering up about *something*! You're working for the Interstate Commerce Commission, scouting for federal offenses such as iron life jackets, leaky lifeboats, wired-down safety valves, and such, right?"

Longarm shook his head and said, "Not hardly. I'm a deputy marshal, not a steamboat inspector. As a general rule I wouldn't know how to go about inspecting a steamboat. But in connection with more serious offenders, I might know more about 'em if I knew more about their methods. How much might you know about that explosion aboard the *Prairie Rose* the other night, Red?"

The local steamfitter sipped at his schooner thoughtfully before he replied. "Just what I've heard. I wasn't there. Knowing the rep of the late Turk Mason, I'd hazard a guess he was steaming at full pressure and change when he ran aground. That's one hell of a time to close your throttle, abrupt, but a lot of pilots do, and a lot of pilots die scalded to death by live steam."

"What about that sternwheeler's safety valve?" asked Longarm. "Are you saying it might have been wired shut, like the one aboard the showboat more recent?"

Red shrugged. "I can't see Turk and Captain Gilchrist going to that much trouble, even if it wasn't a swell way to lose your shipping permit. You'd never tidy things up in time if the steamboat inspectors paid you a surprise visit. But there's more than one way to skin a cat and more than one way to blow up a steam boiler."

"Tell me an easy one," Longarm demanded.

So Red explained. "Safety valves are adjustable. We're talking a good-sized fitting with a spring as big as your forearm and a threaded rod running down through it to adjust the tension."

"How come?" asked Longarm. "Don't any steam boiler explode if it's got too much steam inside with no place to go?"

Red shrugged. "Depends on the rating of the boiler and the size and speed of your engine. Thick boiler plates can safely hold more pressure than thin ones. A big engine running constant for, say, an electicated dynamo can bleed steam almost as fast as even a weak boiler could ever generate it. In sum, each installation calls for such pressure as a licensed steamfitter like myself decides. Nobody'd want to make each and every safety valve to different specifications. So they come in only about a dozen sizes, from penny-whistle to impressive, and we adjust the amount of pressure they'll hold still for by simply turning that threaded valve I just mentioned. The tighter the spring, the more internal pressure it'll take to pop the safety valve, see?"

Longarm swallowed and said, "I do now. You're saying that other steam explosion could have really been the accident it seemed, caused by no more than racing under more pressure than the boilers were rated for until a sudden hike in the pressure made all that noise?"

Red nodded. "I am. You'd have to recover their safety valve to be certain, of course, but like I said, Captain Gilchrist and his pilot both had a rep for pushing hard."

Longarm started to ask a dumb question. He sipped more beer instead. Nobody had to tell him how tough it would be to locate a brass fitting smaller than many a lady's thigh on the muddy bottom of a wide river after it had taken off like that moon ship in that tale by Mister Jules Verne. So he asked, instead, what Red might have heard about the safety record of Captain Gloria Grimes aboard the rival sternwheeler that fatal night.

Red smiled and said he'd done some repair work for Miss Gloria, adding, "No mystery as to why *Morning Star* was out ahead, or why she didn't blow up. The little lady runs a happy ship but a tight ship. I know for a fact every steam fitting aboard the *Morning Star* fits the original plans and specifications of the designer. She don't cut no corners on safety. She just carries no more than her rated load and has her pilot, Jim, steer sensible."

Longarm smiled fondly. "I know. I rode with 'em on another case. In a pinch old Gloria steers pretty good on her own."

Red said it was only natural, Miss Gloria being the daughter of one famous riverboat skipper and the widow of another. So the three of them clinked glasses and then, noting the hour and the number of beers he'd just downed, Longarm parted with them friendly to go scout up some supper.

He chose the dining room of the hotel across from the depot, wishing to know if the hotel was worth checking into if he wound up stuck overnight in Yankton.

The dining room smelled of nothing more sinister than food, drink, and tobacco. It was bug oil you had to sniff for in the vicinity of a strange hotel, and you could always smell it easier mixed with the odors of cooking, because your stomach just didn't want you salivating over anything likely to kill bugs, or you.

But since they hadn't squirted the cracks in recent memory, it seemed safe to assume they had no bugs, or didn't give a damn about bitty red spots on the bed sheets of a morning.

The waitress who served him in a sort of Harvey Gal outfit looked pure Indian.

After supper he went back to the Western Union. His home office hadn't replied to his earlier wire, if they meant to. But to his mild surprise that Ohio insurance company had, informing him with some indignation that they'd never insured any infernal *Prairie Rose,* and that even if they had they'd never yet hired any investigator called Hatfield.

As Longarm put that message away for safekeeping with a curse, the telegraph clerk behind the counter, a nice-looking brunette with big blue eyes, asked if there had been bad news from Cincinnati.

He smiled at her and answered, "Not exactly, ma'am. I never might have wired that home office if I hadn't found it curious that two of their investigators could have made it all the way out here from Cincinnati so sudden."

He saw she still had no idea what he was talking about, so he explained. "I'm riding for the Justice Department, as you

167

must have guessed by now from the wires I've been sending and receiving. The other night a couple of fake insurance dicks questioned me about a steamboat disaster, if that was what they were really interested in. I just found out they were fakes. I'll be dipped in honey and eaten by ants if I can figure what they really wanted to know. Have you ever seen *Uncle Tom's Cabin,* ma'am?"

She hadn't, and better yet, she allowed she'd love to go to the show with him, if only. She didn't get off until midnight, and when she did get off her husband would likely be there to take her home.

But as he was leaving, she told him it had been mighty sweet of him to try. For a lady who'd been married more than two years could always use such assurances. So he assured her she still had her looks as well as his wistful devotion and respect, inspiring her to blush pretty as a rose while costing him nothing but a little white lie about that last part. But Yankton, Dakota Territory, was sure a tough town to get laid in for free.

He knew that whether he met a more willing Yankton gal at a house of ill repute or leaning against the bar in some saloon, she was still likely to laugh at him if he invited her to watch *Uncle Tom's Cabin* with him. So in the end, he moseyed back down to the boat landing alone.

He'd already seen the play, done better, before he'd ever played the part of Simon Legree. His reason for inviting gals from town to go back to the showboat with him, aside from the usual one, was simply that he needed a sensible excuse for going back aboard that showboat. Slipping aboard as a ticket holder, with a gal, required few if any excuses, even if he was recognized amid the crowd. But since that way wouldn't work tonight, he'd just have to tell 'em who he was and what he wanted. For one way or the other, he meant to be aboard until just before they shoved off again, so he could have a gander at the new safety valve after the show, after nobody but a member of the cast or crew could get at it.

Chapter 22

But as things turned out, getting aboard *Fagan's Floating Follies* unobserved was easy. For the showboat wasn't alone at the landing when Longarm returned to the river. The smaller and more businesslike *Morning Star* had just put in, and better yet, a familiar figure with a skipper's cap pinned atop her auburn hair was overseeing the unloading of some buffalo hides she'd brought down out of Montana Territory.

Gloria Grimes took longer to recognize Longarm, dressed as he was, in the tricky light of the boat-landing lamps encircled by bugs under a purple prairie sky. But once she had, after yelling at him to get the blue blazes off her boat till she'd finished and might have time to talk to infernal salesmen, she ran across the cargo deck to give him a friendly hug and sisterly kiss, exclaiming, "Custis Long, you old bastard! I hardly recognized you in that sissy suit! You look like the Prince of Wales, only not as fat and ugly. What are you doing in these parts and how come you run off the last time before I could properly thank you for saving my mail contract as well as my scalp for me?"

He hung on but didn't kiss back, not trusting himself to kiss half as brotherly, as he replied, "Aw, mush. I only done what I was sent to do and my outfit's already thanked

169

me. I'm after other crooks along this river now. How come you're this far down? I figured you'd be up past Milk River by this time, Miss Gloria. Ain't you still running the mail from there upstream where the rails don't run?"

She nodded but said, "Steamboats big as this one don't run halfway to Great Falls with the river half this low either. You recall Jim Truman and my older and smaller *Minnitipi*, don't you?"

He said he surely did. So she explained, "Jim's boating the mail on up right now. This summer we're only running this bigger sternwheeler as far up as Fort Berthold. That's where we picked up those bales of hides, by the by. Seeing they're about unloaded, let's go aft to my quarters and you can tell me what you're doing here whilst I pour."

He said that sounded fair. He had a time recalling just what he'd come down to the river for as he sat on the edge of Gloria's bunk, watching her fuss with the ice pitcher, bottle, and tumblers at her corner cupboard, with her trim back turned to him. He'd forgotten how swell Gloria Grimes filled out a summer-weight officer's tunic and matching skirt, worn Rainy Suzie length to let her move about her decks gracefully, even if it did expose the ankles of her high-button shoes—and nice ankles they were too.

By the time they'd half-finished their drinks he'd brought Gloria up to date on his recent puzzling adventures. She agreed it was a pisser, even if she didn't put it quite that crudely. She'd naturally heard about the *Prairie Rose* blowing up. The news had beaten her to Fort Berthold by wire. She said the news hadn't surprised her. Neither Captain Gilchrist nor Turk Mason had ever had a lick of sense, the steamboat-racing fools.

Longarm couldn't resist asking if she hadn't been racing them at the time of the disaster. She grinned roguishly and asked if it had looked like a race to him.

He grinned back and allowed the *Prairie Rose* had been trailing pretty far back when whatever had happened had happened. When she said it had never been a contest, her having the best boat and pilot, he mused aloud, "Nobody smart enough to figure that would have had any motive to

170

destroy the losing boat then. All anyone betting against the *Prairie Rose* needed to do was do nothing. At the risk of my sounding swell-headed, one steamboat blew up while another almost blew up, with me around both times. So now I want to get back aboard that showboat, sneaky, and see if anyone's still out to sink her."

Gloria frowned thoughtfully before she objected. "Wouldn't that mean they were after somebody else, not you, Custis? I mean, if you're not with those show folk anymore, why would anyone after you be out to hurt any of them?"

He said, "You're learning. What would I have to do to get you to take in the show down the landing this evening?"

She said she'd go just because he asked her. So he rose to his feet, saying, "We'd best get cracking then. I'd like to go aboard with the crowd incognito with a more interesting sight on one arm."

She said she could look even more interesting when she had a mind to, and proved it by whipping off her uniform jacket to accompany him in her well-filled white blouse and perky summer bonnet.

It worked. So once they were seated in the back row of that jury box with a swell view of a whole audience facing the other way, he leaned toward her to whisper, "If they're in cahoots with any member of the cast and crew, they've no reason to be aboard. Nobody else can get to either steam plant save by sneaking around one side or the other of this very chamber."

She whispered back, "I know how a steamboat's laid out. All we have to do is watch for anyone leaving early, right?"

He said, "Not from up here. I got to catch someone doing something before I can do anything about 'em. I'm fixing to hole up out front where I can watch what folk might or might not do as they exit early or late. I'll meet you later aboard your own boat."

Then he slid from his seat before she could object. So on he was out on the bow deck, dying for a smoke, as he lurked in the shadows of the starboard stairs when the entrance of

Simon Legree, inside, was greeted by a chorus of boos, hisses, and at least two shotgun blasts!

So as two familiar figures tore out of the resulting pandemonium with their own sixguns drawn, Longarm simply stepped out of the shadows to throw down on them, yelling, "Drop 'em or die!"

They both skidded to a horrified halt, staring at Longarm as if he had to be a ghost. But neither dropped his gun, so out of respect for his elders, Longarm shot the younger imposter first. As the fake insurance dick staggered back to bounce off the showboat poster for *Uncle Tom's Cabin,* ruining it with a big blotch of gushing gore, the gray-haired one who'd called himself Hatfield was inspired to let go of his gun and warm his hands with the overhead lanterns, wetting his pants and gibbering with terror as his sidekick's dead face beat his gun to the deck at Longarm's feet.

Before Longarm could tell him to quit blubbering, Gloria Grimes tore out to join them, her own bitty garter gun in hand as she pointed it at Hatfield and said, "Don't let him get away! They just shot Simon Legree with a scattergun!"

Longarm nodded pleasantly and replied, "I figured they might have. He ain't getting away, but I'd be obliged if you'd hold back the crowd whilst I march this remaining rascal ashore."

She did her best. But just the same, a modest crowd had gathered about Longarm and his prisoner on the sloping brick landing by the time the Yankton law, local and federal, had responded to the sounds of gunplay. So when one of Marshal Cox's deputies asked how many had been killed, a member of the showboat crew corrected Longarm's first estimate, calling out, "Old Eldrich ain't dead. Just punctuated in less-important parts with buckshot. He brags on having been in the Iron Brigade at Gettysburg and he must have, because you should have seen that old boy duck! Hit the stage and rolled into the wings as the second blast tore right through the place he'd just been!"

Another showboater volunteered, "They carried him to his cabin and the ladies are fussing over him with tweezers and gin."

Longarm didn't ask whether they meant to pour the gin over the old trouper's wounds or down his gullet. He figured neither course of action would really harm Eldrich.

Waving the stubby muzzle of his bulldog at his prisoner, he said, "Neither of the boys sent to gun poor Eldrich need medical attention right now. I'd like to borrow a back room at either the territorial or federal lockup so's me and this one survivor can enjoy a private talk. I'm sure he'd like to tell me who sent him and his late pard to kill me and nobody else but me. You see, gents, that was me they thought they were assassinating just now, and it might have been, had not I been fired as Simon Legree by a lady to whom I'll ever be grateful!"

One of the federal deputies said, "We'd best get him over to our new pokey then." When a town lawman wistfully raised the topic of local jurisdiction Longarm gently told him, "They failed to kill a soul here in Yankton, and meanwhile, we got a multiple murder charge, federal, on this poor cuss. They're still counting the bodies down the river off that steamboat the rascal blew up on a federal waterway."

The Yankton law agreed that had shotgunning an actor's ass beat, but asked if they could watch.

Longarm started to say he liked to work alone in the back room with mass murderers. But on reflection he saw he might not have to use even the threat of such methods, and the more witnesses there were to a confession the harder it was for the rascal to renege in court, after talking to a pesky lawyer.

So leaving just a few Yankton lawmen to keep order at the landing till the town undertaker could tidy up, the rest of them frog-marched Hatfield, if that was his name, the short stroll to the federal house of detention, a frame edifice a tad less imposing than its name.

Sitting Hatfield squarely in the center of a side room, handcuffed to his bentwood chair, Longarm seated himself at a nearby table with a borrowed pad of ruled yellow legal paper, and suggested they start with the prisoner's real name and prior arrest record.

But by this time the piss down Hatfield's right leg had commenced to dry and he had a cruel advantage over Longarm. He knew Longarm's rep. It was widely held along the Owlhoot Trail that while the tall dark deputy from Denver could get mighty lethal, he was a square lawman who didn't go in for either bribes or beatings in back rooms, no matter what he might say. So Hatfield, knowing not even a corrupt copper-badge was likely to really damage a prisoner in front of a mixed bag of witnesses, sat prouder and proclaimed he had nothing to say until he talked things over with his lawyer.

Longarm persisted. "Tell us who your lawyer might be and we'll be proud to send for him by wire, you clever cuss."

It didn't work. Hatfield said he'd settle for any lawyer in Yankton, adding, "I don't need the likes of Daniel Webster to defend me on such charges as you can hope to make stick. Once you question any fair-minded witnesses in that audience back there, you'll find it was that other cuss, not me, who whipped out that sawed-off ten-gauge for whatever reason. I don't have to even attempt to say why. I barely knew the poor lunatic."

Longarm nodded soberly and growled, "Right. It was only natural you'd draw your own pistol as you ran out in panic. Don't bother to tell me you never discharged it or that you dropped it as soon as a peace officer asked you to. I can see where we're headed. I hope you can see I've got you dead to rights on fraudulent impersonation, with witnesses? You identified yourself and that cuss you didn't really know as investigators for an insurance company that never heard of you."

"To what purpose?" countered the prisoner. He added with a knowing sneer, "This very evening a whole cast of actors were pretending to be people they really were not. To fib is only a felony when fraud is intended. Maybe we were just trying to show the owner of that showboat we could act. Did we ask anyone for anything?"

Longarm said, "You did. You asked me all sorts of questions about the destruction of the *Prairie Rose*."

To which Hatfield replied with a superior smile, "I was nosey. How many newspapers would we have in this land if nobody was allowed to ask details about any interesting event?"

One of the other federal men swore under his breath, cracked his knuckles, and said, "Let *me* question the son of a bitch!"

But Longarm shook his head and softly said, "Let's see if I can come up with a better approach." He made a few notes on the pad, tore off the sheet, and handed it to the nearest Yanton lawman with a request to fetch the lawyer indicated. Then he turned back to the obviously wise old owlhoot rider to say, "You're right about what we have on you, for certain. I can't prove the explosion aboard the *Prairie Rose* was deliberate, and we all know that showboat never blew up as planned. So I'll tell you what I'm going to do with you. I'm going to drop the federal charges as soon as you tell me who I'm really mad at. I can't say anything about local ordinances against peppering actors with buckshot. You'll have to work that out with the gent you peppered. He might or might not want to press charges, depending on what you offer and how anxious he is to move on."

Hatfield looked wistful, but shook his gray head, saying, "You know I can't even meet you halfway on that, don't you?"

Longarm smiled back as wistfully, saying, "It was worth a try. I'd like to promise you could talk and walk, but we live in a crowded world. What's to stop the powerful interests you were working for from having you killed before you stand trial? They tried to have *me* killed, didn't they?"

Hatfield nodded soberly and said, "They did, and it was dumb, now that I begin to suspect you never had the least notion of messing things up for 'em."

Longarm said, "I generally have to know who cares before I can judge what they care about. But I follow your drift about the risk of sending a hired gun after a poor simp being held as accessory to flesh wounds. They'd only have to worry about you talking to save your neck if your neck was really likely to stretch."

Hatfield just smiled smugly and asked for a smoke. So Longarm was lighting a cheroot for his prisoner when the Yankton deputy came back in to announce, "Lawyer Gordon's old woman says he had to go over to Mission Hill and might not be back tonight. You want me to see if I can find this cuss another? He's sure going to need a good one, seeing that actor feller just kicked the bucket."

Longarm looked as startled as the prisoner, demanding, "Do tell? I thought he was barely hurt."

To which the local replied with a shrug, "Don't fuss at *me* about it. I ain't no doc and I never shot him, thank God."

This seemed to inspire a mighty morose expression on Longarm's face as he turned his steely gray eyes back to his handcuffed prisoner.

Hatfield licked suddenly dry lips and protested, "Hold on! It was Compton, not me, who fired that buckshot into the poor devil!"

Longarm said, softly, "You know better than that, you lethal legal expert. Whether you pulled the trigger or not, you know who ordered the dirty deed and you're aiding and abetting as long as you refuse to tell us who you hired guns were hired by, and how come."

Hatfield started to protest they'd surely kill him to keep him from talking to save his own neck. Then he noticed how dumb a position that left him in, and proceeded to sing like a canary.

Chapter 23

The moon was still high but the hour was late by the time Longarm made it back to the boat landing. So he wasn't surprised to see both the showboat and Gloria's *Morning Star* blacked out. But he'd told old Gloria he'd come back and explain things as soon as he had the chance, and with Hatfield in a patent cell and his full confession in the office safe of Marshal Cox, he had time to do most anything.

Better yet, a female figure seemed to be standing between him and the gangway of the *Morning Star*. But when he strode closer to say, "I got back soon as I could," he saw it wasn't Gloria Grimes at all. It was Blanche Balmoral, looking a mite contrite and awfully pretty in the moonlight with her pale silk kimono worn so casual. As he doffed his hat to her in confusion she said, "I knew you'd never come back to our showboat. I was hoping against hope I'd catch you here, Deputy Long."

He shrugged and said, "Call me Custis, and don't bother explaining to Brazo, Miss Blanche. A lady has the right to suspect strangers when they act suspicious, and as old Will Shakespeare put it, all's well that ends well. I might have been peppered with buckshot, or worse, if I'd been playing Simon Legree this evening as others had been led to believe I might. How's old Eldrich feeling now?"

She said, "Drunk as a lord. But we got all the pellets out of him. That Simon Legree coat he slipped on over his Saint Clare costume must have helped slow them down quite a bit."

Longarm said, "I'm sure glad to hear that. We just told one of the rascals who peppered him that he'd died. Sometimes you have to fib to fibbers. Nobody was ever after any of you showboaters, Miss Blanche. They were out to kill me because they knew I knew something I didn't. I got to go up that gangway now, if it's all the same with you."

She shook her piled-up curls and pleaded, "Come up my, ah, gangway and tell me all about it, Custis. I'm so confused and we have so much to straighten out between us. . . ."

But Longarm shook his head sadly and replied, "You'll read about it in the papers, ma'am. It'll surely make the front pages across this land once lawmen all up and down the river round up the dozen or more villains deeply involved."

She insisted, "That's not all we have to straighten out between us."

But he wasn't sure how one got it straight enough to matter with a lady as confused about such matters as this one sounded, even if he'd wanted to. So he ducked around her and headed for Gloria's cabin whether the pretty young widow had her own kimono securely fastened or not.

As it turned out, Gloria Grimes was still in her blouse and skirt when she headed him off in the dimly lit companionway. She murmured, "Keep it down. I've some sleeping passengers. Who was that hussy who wanted you to sleep with her just now?"

Longarm chuckled softly and replied, "Little Eva. I didn't think she slept with boys of any description. But she just said she was a mite confused. Do you want to gossip about things that never happened or would you like me to tell you, at last, what was happening up and down the Big Muddy all this time?"

She led him into her cabin, sat him down, and began to build drinks for the two of them again as he explained. "In the beginning I was sent after a federal want called Lucky

178

Lovelace. He'd left Cairo after killing another federal agent. Whether he left aboard this vessel or another, he later wound up aboard the *Prairie Rose,* so—"

"I never had anyone named Lovelace come aboard at Cairo," she said, interrupting.

Which inspired him to growl, "I just told you he was aboard the *Prairie Rose* all the time that mattered. This'll take too long if we pause to pick over every infernal nit."

She handed him his drink and sat down beside him, assuring him she was all ears. He thought some other parts of her stuck out more interestingly, but didn't say so as he continued. "I may never be able to say for sure which one of the nondescript gents I met aboard the doomed *Prairie Rose* was really Lucky Lovelace. Suffice it to say he spotted *me.* That's the trouble with having a certain rep after riding six or eight years for the Justice Department. Anyway, he jumped me from behind and lost his own life whilst saving mine, albeit I doubt that could have been his intention at the time."

He sipped his drink, blinked when he noticed how strong she'd built it, and went on. "Forget the case Billy Vail had sent me on, once the cuss I was seeking wound up catfish grub. I didn't know my man was dead, for certain, so I went on playing things close to my vest in this sissy disguise Bill Vail sent me out to play in. That made the owners of the *Prairie Rose* wonder what in thunder I could be up to. I mean, what would you think if someone told you a federal agent was pussyfooting about amid your passengers without letting on who he was?"

She thought, shrugged, and answered, "A lawman closing in on one or more of my passengers, or failing that, a steamboat inspector. They're always sneaking aboard to catch us in some violation, speaking of nit-picking."

Longarm nodded and said, "Steamboat racing with your safety valves too tight for the rated pressure of your boilers is more than a nit, ma'am. It's good for a hearing before the interstate commerce board."

She shrugged. "If anyone could make it stick. Jim Truman and me were racing more sensible that night, if you'll

179

remember, but who's to say whether we were really racing or how we had our valves adjusted? Even if you had had the goods on Captain Gilchrist and his notorious crew, what could the commerce board have done to them, once they were all dead, revoke their papers?"

"That's what the owners of the blown-up boat must have been sweating bullets about, once they noticed I was still pussyfooting about in this sissy suit pretending to be a simple soul who'd survived the explosion. They figured I'd caught on to 'em, escaped by the skin of my teeth, and was working undercover to get more on 'em."

"More of *what*?" she demanded impatiently.

So he got right to it by telling her, "Mass murder—or the liquidation of an unprofitable business enterprise, as they likely justified it among themselves. I surely don't have to tell a lady in the twilight time of steamboating how tough it's gotten to show a profit running a paddle wheeler unless you know exactly what you're doing."

She frowned. "I know exactly what I'm doing, but Jacob Gilchrist was a careless cuss."

Longarm nodded. "They bought the *Prairie Rose* at what they mistook for a bargain, spruced her up, and sent her out to make 'em some bucks under a skipper and pilot known mostly for winning races because they were running light as well as reckless. Despite all her fancy trimmings, or mayhap because of 'em, the *Prairie Rose* was losing money for her owners every trip. Meanwhile they'd insured her and all that fancy gingerbread heavy, so—"

"No wonder she blew up that night!" Gloria said, interrupting, staring at him aghast. "But can you prove someone doctored her steam plant to blow no matter what poor Gilchrist and his crew might do?"

He said, "We don't have to. Hatfield's confessed in full detail. He'd had us believe it was his more silent partner, Compton, who made and planted a time bomb under the boiler of the *Prairie Rose* and wired the safety valve aboard the showboat in hopes of covering the one crime with another. You see, when they learned the sole survivor of the first planned explosion seemed to be working undercover for the

180

federal government, they added two and two to get a comedy of errors going."

She finished her drink and rose to refill her glass and freshen his as she said, "I can see why. A federal steamboat inspector could have caused them enough trouble with their insurance claims. When you went on working undercover instead of reporting the late Jacob Gilchrist's reckless behavior, they figured you hadn't bought the explosion as the accident they were trying to sell."

Longarm sipped, blinked at the kick she'd put in his replenished glass, and said, "Yep. All their sneaky moves make sense once you study on how little sense I must have been making to them. I wasn't even thinking about who might or might not own a sunken steamboat as I floundered about fretting about a wanted killer who was already dead and a lady in peril who was never in peril to begin with."

Gloria raised a brow. "Oh? I might have known there'd be another woman involved. How was she in bed, you horny rascal?"

Longarm met her eyes, innocently, as he replied, "That wasn't what I was worried about. A gal who'd told me she was a private detective tracking down a fortune hunter who'd robbed a rich widow from Texas scared me good by leaving for Texas in the company of the very man she claimed to be hunting. I thought he might have had the drop on her. But Billy Vail had some of the boys straighten out the confusion when the happy couple passed through Town. I just got the word on that when I wired the news about tonight to Denver."

"Happy couple?" asked Gloria with a puzzled frown.

So Longarm nodded and explained. "She was the wealthy widow he'd bilked, as well as a gal with a Texas hunting license who meant to show him what for. But as it turned out, he'd never done her dirty at all. They'd just gotten their hotels in Omaha mixed up. He'd been hunting high and low for her as well, with some *dinero* he owed her. So things turned out swell for, ah, all concerned."

She said, "Oh, for a moment I thought you'd made another conquest."

181

He looked hurt. "How come you ladies always accuse me of such vile intentions? Did I ever make a play for you that time we first met aboard the old *Minnitipi*, Miss Gloria?"

She set her glass aside and fixed him with a smoldering look as she demurely replied, "You did not. And that's a bone I've been meaning to pick with you ever since."

Watch for

LONGARM AND THE DENVER BUST-OUT

149th in the bold LONGARM series
from Jove

Coming in May!